I WILL LOVE ONCE AGAIN!

....no matter how much I still miss you

I WILL LOVE ONCE AGAIN!

....no matter how much I still miss you

Krishna

Srishti
PUBLISHERS & DISTRIBUTORS

SRISHTI PUBLISHERS & DISTRIBUTORS
N-16, C. R. Park
New Delhi 110 019
srishtipublishers@gmail.com

First published by Srishti Publishers & Distributors in 2012
Copyright © Krishna, 2012

ALL MAJOR CHARACTERS IN THIS NOVEL ARE 100% FICTITIOUS ANY
RESEMBLANCE TO ANYONE LIVING, DEAD OR TO BE BORN IS PURELY
COINCIDENTAL

Typeset in AGaramond 12pt. by Suresh Kumar Sharma at Srishti

I may not tell her so in words,
Doesn't mean I don't love her.
I think of her each and every moment,
But I don't want to admit it.
With struggling days, sleepless nights
I still cry for her and miss our fights.
You went far away from me,
I am still looking for you in agony.
Running here and there in pain,
I promise 'I will fall in love once again'.

Acknowledgements

Writing this book was a tribute to my love and there are so many people that I am overwhelmed with gratitude.

I am thankful to my Parents and sister for their love and support. My special thanks to priety without whom this book would not have been there. Thanks for being in my life, wherever you are I am sure you would be glad as I kept my promise. APJ school and my great teachers who always supported me during my challenging phase and assisted me in completing my schooling. My college DAVIET and my evergreen college friends Ridhi, Deepti, Aseem, Rupali and shiven. My cutest junior Priyanka kakkar who recently got married.

Thanks to WIPRO technologies, My ex tech leads Isha gupta and Bindya Sharma for believing in me. My ex manager Ramit Kumar who always guided and stood behind me. Chiya(Pooja) my ex Wipro acquaintance and first to ever know that I will be writing.

Richa bajaj and Prateeksha aggarwal who are always with me and promised to promote my book. My manager Hitesh jain for being my wall. My friends Saurabh singh, Kamal, Deepika Arora.

Thanks to Varun Maria for reviewing every page and for always believing in me that I can be the Star, Simerdeep singh bhatti for being such a character that I can bank on and for always believing in me that I can do anything, Puneet Sharma for all the great time in Pune and his assistance forever.

Special thanks to Sharika for being so unique and for her critics and then her prayers & wishes for me. Rakshandha for her prayers especially during the phase when I needed them the most. Aishwarya kothapali for always praying, encouraging and wishing me.

Thanks to my maternal relatives for supporting us during my

toughest phase, Sachal babbar for motivations, prayers, wishes and all the good things I keep learning from him.

Srishti publishers for being so encouraging and promoting my writing.

OM SHANTI

CALL LETTER AND JOINING

March 2009:

"*I got engaged. The guy is nice, earning handsomely and has a family business as well.*"

"*Are you happy?*" *I asked her.*

"*My family is happy.*" *She responded.*

"*Congratulations!*" *I could say only this and she disconnected the phone.*

I completed my B.Tech in Information Technologies from DAVIET in 2008, that too with distinction. The year was 2008-09 which every engineering student would want to erase out from their memory. The recession landed many people with cut offs in their salaries, pink slips in their pockets and never ending hope for the campus placement. That was the time when many parents might have been thinking of engineering as a curse. I too have reasons to hate the same year but different ones. After a series of failures in my attempt to run my own business and having lost the girl whom I loved since 12th standard, I flunked in all the marketing concepts that I tried to achieve something big and like every bollywood movie my girl. It was the time when I felt like a destitute and like every other normal guy held God responsible for everything. Right from taking away my girl to making me face the loss in my business, I lost all trust on that supreme power; I packed all the images, in my room and dumped them into a box. I had no option left but to explore classified columns of the local newspapers to search for jobs matching my profile.

It does happen that sometimes you lose all your hopes but suddenly there is a surprise for you something most unusual and unexpected. I waited for a year and then finally got a call from an MNC. I got this mail on 4th April 2009 which was as follows:

Dear,

We acknowledge and appreciate your patience in waiting to join our organization. We are also eagerly looking forward to have your on board with us. We are committed to honor every offer that is made and it gives us pleasure to communicate your date of joining.

Your joining date is scheduled on 22nd Sep 2009

Details of joining formalities and location of in-house training would be communicated two weeks in advance from the above date of joining.

The details of the induction and engagement program are as follows:

In house Training:

• *You would be in an in-house training for a period for 2 months, as per your offer letter.*

Month in lieu of salary. Your salary (as per your offer letter) will be restored once a suitable project opportunity has been identified for you and you have commenced working on the same.

We also take this opportunity to convey to you that in view of the delay in joining we have decided to make an exception and waive off the Bond formality for campus selects of 2008 batch that will be joining us post April 1, 2009.

• *On successful completion of your training you would be assigned to projects with salary as per your offer letter.*

It is possible, however, due to the difficult market conditions currently prevailing, that we may not be able to assign you to a suitable project immediately on completion of the in-house training. Should such a situation arise, we would engage you actively through an extended Web based training program at residence, which will be delivered by company's Talent Transformation team. While you are on extended training, you will be paid an interim allowance of Rs.6000 per

Yours sincerely,

Well! Unexpected surprise never means all that things will be under your control. The e-mail above had some favorable news and bad news too. The good news waived us all from any bond with the company but the bad one was that now the company could kick us anytime because of no bond. The good news stated that the package would be same as per the offer letter but sadly due to bitter market conditions we might be sent back with only training programs in our pocket.

Now the question was to sit and wait for the September joining as it could be delayed in future depending upon the marketing conditions or to move forward and join local companies here and there. My maternal aunts and neighbours were already preparing their children for the future by giving my example of completing my studies and still sitting home. Who would explain recession to them or make them understand that I was not sitting at home out of my own sweet will after 4 years of exasperating studies. So to shut them up and to keep myself occupied I joined some private firm as a software consultant on incentive bases! What an irony! The guy who just passed out would be a consultant and that too for the products he should be developing. But it was hundred percent a marketing job tagged with consultant on the visiting card.

I now decided to lead a life where I would let it take complete charge. No expectations, no enthusiasm, no energy and no life. I was already shattered, unlike a few months back when I was running my own business and my girl was with me. I was then leading life on the edge, charging everyday with the energy to create something big and achieving her but in a split second the game turned and I was here.

I had a dream boss in the company I joined. He was smart, Intelligent, witty and cooperative but nobody is perfect so he had a weakness too and that was a glad eye for the beautiful hot girls in the office. He used to remind me of an amazing character played by Aditya Pancholi in YES BOSS.

"We are developing software that will allow them to keep track of each and every patient in a hospital. I hope you get it and the next time you target clients with the same requirement. Preet will hand over all the details to you." My boss explained.

Preet was my boss's personnel assistant or you can say another consultant like me handling marketing job. She was just a girl of 18 and pursuing her BCA degree on a distant learning programme. Technically she was my senior too.

"May I come in?"

Our eyes shifted to the door in the cabin as it was a soft voice, possibly that of a girl. She was Neha a new recruit. She not only entered the room but directly into my boss's heart..

"You can leave now as I guess you have an appointment." Smilingly my boss waved at me. I had no option just to obey him.

I came late the next morning, so he was the first person I met.

"Why so late?"

I was running short of a specific reason so I replied quickly,

"I had a meeting with the principal."

"Oh! So how was it?"

"It was good and they may opt for our services." I smiled.

"I hope this client of yours opts for our services like your previous client did." My boss replied sarcastically. "I hope you come in time from tomorrow."

I left the cabin and went to my bay where the team was already present, staring at me as if I was answerable to them. To my surprise, my seat was already occupied and Neha was working on my PC. I quietly went and sat near her.

A formal introduction and we started chatting. It does happen that sometimes you get close to some people very soon and sometimes you take ages. I never understood this philosophy of positive vibes or negative ones, but soon we were talking. As we talked I never knew that how time passed and it was lunch. But before that I got a call on my intercom.

"So I hope your deal is fixed?" Inquired the voice from other side.

"Who's this?" I asked softly.

"Your damn boss!!!!"

"Oh boss! I stood up, Sir I was about to leave and I thought I will…"

"What you will? Don't just sit and enjoy the office AC, just go out and enjoy the work too."

Beep! Beep!

I smiled, pretending to be normal and confidently said, "My client is impatient to see me."

"I guess it was your boss Na." She asked inquiringly.

I was left with no choice but to leave and go out for the deals. I don't know why all bosses and managers are given the right to peep into their junior's personal life. My boss was looking me from the cabin as my bay was just opposite.

I was not at all serious about the job I was in but somehow I managed to close one or two deals and my boss was really happy with me. My interaction with the team was good and Neha also joined it. We used to lunch together, have tea and even left the office at the same time. As the days passed this became one of the reasons that my boss started to keep an eye on me. Anytime, anywhere if I was seen talking to her, I always get a call from him. Who wouldn't? Especially if you are planning to marry the same girl with whom your junior is going around. But my boss was not that rude, he used to make comments, some sarcastic remarks but more often they were in a friendly way. May be he was sure there was nothing between two of us or he knew that after all he was the boss.

Everything was going fine, being an engineer I was doing well in the marketing job, thanks to the earlier experience where I had failed miserably. The office was good and my acquaintances were very nice to me, but somewhere in my mind there was something that was making me insecure and uncomfortable. I was not at all at the right job. I was able to engage myself completely during the day but was going through the struggling sleepless nights as I cried and constantly mourned the past. I wanted to run away, far away from this city. It could be anywhere, any corner around the world but it should not be Jalandhar. Each day seemed like climbing the mountain, moreover half my mind was always glued to the cell phone. Everyday I got up and morning seemed to be so heavy on me, the past always flashed hard during the sunrise and that too with powerful intensity that left me with the agony and pain of losing her. The only hope that seemed to me was the MNC call letter and that was still on my mind and I was heading close to September but still no final intimation from them. Would they call me? What if they didn't? Will I stick to the job where I am just on incentive basis? Oh recession! Why the hell did you have to come at this time?

Finally all my questions were answered when I was sent a final call for the September. I was supposed to report on 17 September at Pune. There were reasons to cheer and there few glitches too. My other batch mates were asked to join in Bangalore together but I alone was thrown to Pune, land of swine flu as most of the news channels were busy highlighting every hour. I knew nobody there, how would I manage?

On the other end it was a shocker for everyone in my company that I was leaving on 13 September and my boss offered me a handsome package and a proper post so that I could rethink my decision of resignation. But an MNC was something else as the brand name says all. So I rejected my boss's offer. Oh Jesus! How great is the feeling when you reject something like this. My work was appreciated not only by my boss but by the seniors of other department as well, I didn't know why. My farewell was arranged with a cake and all and every member of the company joined me at the cafeteria on my last day. Everybody congratulated me as if I had been offered post of the CEO and before leaving I gifted my boss with the CD of the film YES-BOSS. He had never seen that film and I always told him

"Sir! You resemble the hero of the film."

It was the last night and I was thinking of her. Priety was my life, my dream and my love. 'Priety' was the name that had greatest impact and dominated my heart for span of seven long years and still did. I had met her during my school days and had never ever thought that this classy beauty with a magnetic aura would take charge of my life.

It was not love at first site but it was friendship which was overwhelmed by love and that too so spontaneous and unplanned that I lost my heart and surrendered everything when I realized that it was too late and I was trapped in the purest relationship of my life. She was the one for whom my heart beat fast, she was the person for whom I wanted to be something great in life, she was the one for whom I always loved my cell phone and kept myself glued to it expecting it to flash her number every time. She was the one for whom I always believed of turning anything from impossible possible. She was reason behind my happiness, my glow, my charm and my life. The moments spent with her were all haunting me the last few hours before I could leave for a new place. How would I survive there without her? How would I resist myself from calling her? Why did this happen to me? Why had life become so harsh when I expected it to be better?

There were many questions that bothered me and I felt helpless as if I had been left alone in the middle of a lonely desert. It just happens when life brings such an unusual moment of which you never ever thought especially ruling out the one whom you loved more than you, leaving you cursing, crying and lonely confined to the four walls of your past where it just haunts you and makes every second unbearable for you. But the fact is you have to survive and wait for the tide of the toughest time to turn. I was doing the same as well as consoling myself giving all the valid and supportive reasons to cheer up and focus on the task ahead, that of surviving in the new place.

The whistle of the engine was loud and clear, the signal was green and I waved a final goodbye to my parents. I could see the tears in my mother's eyes though she was hiding them. After all how can I forget those expressions as they were the same as they used to be when I was being dropped to school in upper KG's? She knew that this year I suffered two of the major bruises my own business debacle and my love, so she was bit extra concerned that I may or may not be able to cope up with.

Whenever one loses love ones in life there are two options left, either one goes mad, lamenting all the time, brooding and wasting time on the past, completely ruining one's life, the other option is to keep oneself busy, get involved in work, going and partying with friends and never ever fall in love again but I choose the third option and that was to try and find love once again. I remember the *Love Aaj Kal* dialogue, *'mujhe kam se kam 15 baar hua hai paaji'* If he could then I can also find love again at least half a dozen times. Ya I had to be bit optimistic now.

The retired Colonel on berth number 21 wished me good morning. I just got up after a short nap and checked my cell for messages from Priety. I guess that was the last message from her. Oh I was missing her again. It is tough to get rid of the past sometimes no matter how many promises you make to yourself. I remember how she always used to call and message whenever I went out of station. She would keep on wishing me safe journey and to be careful as if I would be driving the train. All that was behind me now, like a dream.

"So where are you going young boy?" Asked the Colonel looking at me and sipping the morning tea.

"Pune!" I replied.

"So you study?"

"No I am going for a job."

I told him about the offer I had got. After a few minutes I came to know more about him. After serving the army for so many years he was happily returning to Pune after a holiday in Kashmir, Himachal and Punjab. He was a proud man, very intelligent with a good general knowledge. He knew 5 Indian languages and being from Army background he seemed to analyze things carefully with each and every possible approach to handle everything.

"Why don't you try for a job in the army?" He asked.

I was expecting this question as it was not the first time I had been asked to join the army or navy. I remember how my uncle challenged me to go and get selected when I refused to give SSB interview after clearing the first round for the army during the last semester of college. He was very angry and fired me left and right.

Actually I couldn't tell my uncle that Priety hated army officers; a guy in love can always change professions, reject fabulous offers and could mould his career according to the wishes of the charming girl he courted. I might be wrong but who cares, I was in love with her.

"I am not interested as I feel my country needs me somewhere else other than the borders. And I can earn well in the corporate world." I replied softly. He frowned.

"So you feel that you are not interested. I don't know what is the damn problem with the youth today is. Why they are reluctant to serve the country? Why do they run after money blindly? The youth today just find reasons to run away from their responsibilities."

I could see the repeat telecast of what had happened earlier when my uncle had blasted for not going for the SSB. Why are all army and navy people same? I was wondering whether they were trained together. For a moment I thought that he might know my uncle but then I reminded myself that he was in the navy. What if they had met during the 26th January Parade at some point of time?

The colonel shifted to gear four.

"You just look at my salary, even after retirement I am getting 80k, ration and other facilities. What else do you need in life?"

I kept on nodding with my eyes wide open, eye brow raised and an expressions as if I agreed everything to he said.

We remained quiet for about three hours and finally T.N Shiva ram broke the silence asking the colonel to let him know about the procedure to join the army. T.N was a medical student pursuing his degree from Karnataka. A typical south Indian guy, a bit reserved, shy and polite.

I felt this was the best opportunity to bring him back to the same mode as I needed to ask him many things about Pune so I immediately jumped into the conversation and said "Yes uncle! What exactly is the criterion for SSB?" I tried to show all the interest I could.

That seemed to bring the smile back on his face. The feeling of joy and pride was evident in his voice now. He explained the entire procedure and interviewed us very earnestly. The questioning round continued from Agra Cant railway station up to Jhansi. He was convinced that I can join the army as I would clear the rounds and can be a perfect fit. Finally at Jhansi I was free. The trick to get information about Pune resulted in about of giddiness but I virtually got selected in the army.

After that we had talked casually. I asked a few things about Pune. At 10 o clock we reached Bhopal. A guy came in with so much luggage that he blocked the entire passage.

"Hi Jatin here, I am a lawyer and going for further studies to London university." He said in an American accent.

From his accent and dressing sense I could judge that he was an over confident person. Before leaving Jalandhar I was well aware that I would have to encounter such guys every now and then. One who was leaving his hometown for the first time would always have thought that the big cities were full of proud, snobbish and repulsive people.

We introduced each other, Colonel uncle as lively as he was in the morning and Jatin were now talking and they both had a great chat and that too in English. T.N slept in between as he was not interested in the conversation but I couldn't as the volume was so high it seemed as if they were fighting.

Just shut up! What the hell you guys think of you? I wanted to say this, but couldn't.

I was thinking of what could be done to change the mode of conversation or just to make them shut up. Finally that chance came.

"What are your views about this?" The colonel asked me.

What views? What topic? I was hardly listening to them. Rather than asking again about the topic they were discussing and giving an answer to the question I didn't know I finally said.

"Hey uncle it seems that you are a typical Virgo character and Jatin seems to be Libran. I am really impressed by both of you. What a chat you had. I enjoyed myself like I never had earlier." I replied.

"Hey how come you know that I am a Libran?" Jatin asked astonished.

But this time his accent was more or like an Indian. Before I could answer his question, the colonel uncle admitted to be a Virgo as well.

For Jatin it was very simple, I saw his date of birth when he was showing his ID proof to the Ticket checker and for uncle it was just a confident guess. Priety used to show a lot of interest in sun signs; she was specific sometimes and always tried to judge people on the basis of their sun signs. In my initial days I read the whole of Linda Good man to impress her. A book especially written on sun signs. A guy has to do a lot to impress a girl, I could have done better in my academics rather than reading that 500 plus pages book. I don't know whether she got impressed or not but the sun sign formula always worked with other girls and at that moment Jatin and colonel uncle were keen to know more about their sun signs.

So till the time they all went to sleep it was all I who was telling them about them confidently.

The next day the train reached Pune. By that time I had developed a few good contacts that could be handy for me in Pune as kernel uncle and Jatin provided me with enough databases of their close friends who could assist me. I got a call on my cell just when I came out of the station.

"*Oh kidda? Ki haal hai tera?* "

"Hello! Who's this?"

"Shiven here! I came to know that you are coming to Pune. When will you be here? Do let me know, I am in Pune."

"Oh Shiven, you are in Pune!" I replied a bit shocked.

Shiven had been my classmate during college days, a very lively guy with a great sense of humour and a bit philosophical too in a peculiar way. He was in Pune and working in an MNC, he gave me his address and I was relieved.

The auto rickshaw guys heard the address when I was talking to my friend. A few of them started to pick my bag up trying to persuade me to sit in their auto. I guess they can easily judge who the new guy in the town was. One quicker than others, he greeted me and tried to tell me about the place where I was supposed to go.

"Arre sir, jo theek lage dedena. Just sit sir."

Finally I took an auto to Bhaudan where my friend's flat was. We never decided on the fare as he kept on talking about silly things that I was hardly interested in. I tried to ask him many times about the fare and meter reading but he was quick in changing the topic shrewdly.

"Arrey bhaiya! Let me know the rough idea about the fare till Bhaudan."

"Sir Rs 400 only."

"Oh Rs 400, shabash! Stop the damn auto right here." I shouted. In 400 I can travel 4 times from Jalandhar to Chandigarh.

"Oh sahib this is Pune not Chandigarh." He replied.

He stopped the auto at Pashan road and I took my luggage and got of it.

"Now I see how you get money from me. I am standing here. I know you damn auto drivers. How you try to plunder the money from the new guys in town." Pointing my finger towards him I said aggressively.

"*Oh sahib! Ungli neeche rakho*? You don't know who I am." We were on the point of quarrelling when finally Shiven called and asked me about the place I got stuck.

He came and resolved the issue. Finally I paid just Rs 75 as per the meter and still don't know how my friend calculated the fare. May be he had gone through such situations many times.

I reached his place and met a few other friends from my college at Shiven's place. Oh it was great to see them all after one whole year. I had lost all the contact with them after college. We were exchanging notes about all the good times we had and finally at 11 pm Shiven took me out for ride. He had beer and a cigarette on the way and asked me to drive. We drove to Sus road. It was a lovely place but only if you were with your partner. I could see some of the couples sitting there and getting naughty with each other. The only thing we could do was to ignore them. On such occasions one either feels jealous or find faults with the couple concerned. Who cares whether they were having fun?

The view from that point was great at night; the buildings were glowing in the light. It felt great to see it and like a typical bollywood movie hero I raised my head high and hands sideways.

"I will buy these buildings one day." I said affirmatively

I was expecting a graceful response from my friend who was looking at me with right eyebrow raised, a beer in left hand and cigarette in right. He took one puff and blowing out the smoke said.

"I am drunk; I don't know why you are barking pointlessly. Come down and have a drink you recently employed idiot."

"I don't drink." I said aggressively.

"Then let me drink in peace."

I came down and sat near him wondering why I had said what I had.

The office which I was supposed to join was at Hinjewadi phase-1. The new employees were asked to report on 17th September. So I inquired everything about how to reach the place. It was my first day in an MNC. I could see the bunch of fresh faces like mine, enthusiastic as well as nervous. They were all standing in a queue at the gate so as to get their documents checked and get a temporary gate pass.

I was thinking about 10th march, 2007 at my college when my name had been announced with that of others who had got selected in.

Priety had been messaging me constantly and waiting for my call as she had instructed me strictly to let her know first about the good news.

Immediately I pulled out my cell and was going to dial her number when friend called to know the result and he talked for 15 minutes. Sometimes you get right calls at wrong time and you are helpless…

I found fifteen missed calls and I knew she would take ages to pick my call. Finally the 31'st call was picked up by her.

"Priety! I am sorry. I got selected a friend called and then ….."

"Congratulations!" She interrupted and said as if she was throwing a stone at me.

I couldn't say even thanks as that would make her disconnect the call. So I tried to say 'I am sorry' in a passive tone and that worked a bit before she exploded.

"You always ignore me like this. When I asked you to call me first, why the hell didn't you? You must be talking to anjali."

Anjali was my junior and I had once said just that she was the hottest girl amongst the juniors.

That was enough to convince Priety that I might be talking to her from time to time.

Oh God! What a fertile imagination girls can have.

"No Priety it was Aseem. My friend and he happens to be a boy."

I loved it when she got possessive like this but somebody reminds her that it was a great day for me, I was in an MNC now. It took me three hours to make her believe that it was Aseem's call before I got a kiss on the phone and congratulations in a soft tone. Thanks to an offer letter, my kiss on phone.

I got down from the bus and joined the queue. I recognized a few faces from my college, though we were not from the same department. A few of them waved at me as I guessed they recognized me; so I joined them.

"Hey! How come you are here? "Shubleen asked." And how are you?" Dilpreet joined. Shubleen and Dilpreet were my school and college mates but from different departments.

"Ih ithe churan vechan aya hai (He is here to sell some digestive pills) Idiot! Obviously he is new like us." Simer said in a typical Punjabi accent. Everybody laughed.

Simerdeep Singh was a unique character He was a slim and smart Sikh boy from Amritsar, popularly known as Singh Khan during his college days as he used to mimic Shah Rukh Khan uniquely in his own Punjabi way. Wherever you found people laughing you would find him standing and cracking some jokes.

We moved in as it was the happiest moment in one's life to be in such a big company that too after the tsunami of recession.

Is this an office? We were all amazed because till then, for us office was just like a cabin or a multi storey building with a few good floors. But this was something else. It was as if we were in some university campus, with well maintained lawns on both sides of the passage, the buildings standing tall behind the trees. The parking lot nearby was packed with cars. There were many buildings and we were asked to report at Platinum hall which was supposed to be the part of Building-2. We could see the senior employees with their ID cards around their necks staring at us just the way seniors in the college had done. For a moment I thought they might start ragging us.

Do people actually come here to work? How can people work in such a lively environment? Are these buildings empty? Oh god what a crowd! What a view! What a building!

We all were in at 10 AM sharp as per the time which we were asked to report. There were around 60 trainees in the room. The room was more or less like the convention hall. There were people from different parts of the country. The whole scenario seemed to be the same as it had been years back on the first day of college, but this time we wouldn't be paying, instead we would be paid. How exciting it was.

"Good morning everyone and welcome to our organization." Somebody greeted us. We were so occupied that we didn't even notice that lady from HR department was already in the room.

"I am Shallu Kapoor. And before I tell you about the further proceedings I would like to be introduced to all of you."

The round of introduction was followed up by that of document verification. We were filling up the form gladly, having our documents verified when we were introduced to Mr. Chirag, head HR. He was supposed to be the one who would guide us all through the company's policies and guidelines, rules and regulations, dos and don'ts and most importantly acquaint us with the company's integrity issues. I know that sounds a bit technical. After greeting, he handed us forms stating the fact that we could be asked to work from home after training if we were unable to find a project. Though we were not willing, we had to sign that form.

Company would categorize us on the basis of our performance based on the tests we would be taking. There would be BIN1 reserved for toppers, BIN2 for mediocre and BIN3 for the guys who will be hanging on the finishing line. I was already thinking of the BIN3, as there are something's in life you are so confident of achieving successfully.

Then we were called in alphabetical order to submit our documents and collect the temporary pass. My turn came and I was handed the card and the hook to bind it. I never even checked my name but my eyes turned to the number written on it on the right hand corner. It was 47, the number that had been on my mind for the last few years. It was Priety's college roll number. Being in love, I was in the habit of looking for that number everywhere, in phone numbers, number plates or even the marks I used to get in the college thinking that the more I saw the number the stronger my love would be. I know it seems weird but I loved that number.

Lost in my thoughts I was walking down. Something was hurting in my hand and I just threw it in the dustbin nearby. There was a pin drop silence in the hall. I realized I had thrown that hook into the dustbin. I went to the dustbin so that I could pick it up but everybody was staring at me. I went to HR and I asked for another one and she handed it to me.

"Where are you from?" She asked.

"I am from Punjab."

"Oh that's why! All Punjabis are like that." She said and smiled.

What do you mean all are like that? But I couldn't ask her that. Instead I went to my seat quietly ignoring everyone.

Later we came out for lunch and discussed accommodation trying to choose stalemates and was pairing up with each other. I didn't want to stay far in Bhaudan. So I asked Simer.

"Yar I am looking for a girl." Simer replied, sounding preoccupied.

"A girl! For what?" I asked.

"Yes a girl who would be comfortable with me in living relationship."

"Oh wonderful! Even I would prefer it. Don't you think it's hard to find a girl in a day?" I said smilingly.

"Great man! Our thoughts match, no matter how pathetic they are." He giggled.

He was right. If not thoughts our natures matched in certain ways, the vibes matched. Finally we decided to postpone the idea of a live-in relationship to move with one of Simer's friends living in Kalewari Fata.

He introduced me to him.

"Hi I am Varun. You can join us and I guess you won't have any problem as we are already three guys living in a 2 BHK"

"No problems *veer*. Now we would be five." Simer interrupted.

Varun had been in the same MNC for one year. He was a guy from Ludhiana and to my surprise he was from my college only and Simer's classmate. How strange that I had never met Simer and Varun during my college days but now I would be sharing accommodation with them. He was an intelligent guy technically very sound, very friendly by nature.

"Thanks a lot Varun. I will join you guys on 21st. I would leave for Goa tonight to be with my maasi." I replied.

GOA

I left the company directly for Swar Gate as I needed to catch the bus from there. I had done this to avoid getting late; instead I reached 2 hours early at the point from where my bus was supposed to depart. I had gone to Goa earlier in 2007, I had had a big fight with Priety a day before I was supposed to leave. If I say I had a fight it means that I was a mere listener tagged with the responsibility of initiating the fight. I called her after my last exam of 6th semester during our college days.

"Hello! How was the exam?" She asked.

"Hey my angel. Exam was good as I ….."

Before I could continue she started to describe her own exam, how she had handled the paper, how just at the last minute she had thought of an answer, how tactically she had answered the question that confused her. She forgot about my reply to her question. But I did not mind it as I was used to such interruptions and lack of interest because she was always running with excitement to tell me about the things she did. I used to feel a bit hurt but I never showed it. After all who would pay attention to my boring exam. That was not enough; I had to appreciate her intelligence and show glumness when she missed a difficult question.

"That's wonderful. My love is so intelligent. How cleverly you solve everything! I am amazed, so now you would score good marks." I appreciated.

"No yar, but I missed a few questions, I am worried whether I could even get pass marks." She added.

"Oh ho! How many questions did you miss dear?" I asked worriedly.

"There were 4 questions I doubt."

"Oh no Priety!"

"Two were 2 mark question and one was for 4 marks. I could write only for about 2 pages but I think I could have elaborated some more. There was one 6 mark question, which I am not so confident if it was correct, I discussed it with my lecturer and she supported the same reason I gave but I still….." She replied innocently and paused.

Nonsense! I felt like kicking the wall. Somebody tell her that I have left both the 6 mark questions as I didn't read a few chapters, the 2 mark questions were always tricky so I never bothered to waste time on them. How would I pass? But if I let her know the same she would yell at me saying that I should study properly. "I hate people failing in the exams", she would add. What could I say to her? I could think of nothing suitable.

"Please don't worry you are sure to score good marks my topper." I said.

"Alright, alright. Hey I am planning to meet you this Saturday as we have not met for the last two months. I can come to your place." She replied excitedly.

"My place! This Saturday? But I told you that I would be leaving for Goa to my maasi's place for 15 days." I replied.

"A few minutes silence and then she exploded. "When the hell did you tell me that? You always spoil my mood. I tell you each and everything but you always hide things from me. Get lost!"

Beep! Beep! Beep!

I remembered I had told her twice but she was always so preoccupied, so lost in her thoughts that she forgot. She often did that, blaming me for not letting her know my plans even if I had. Actually she was the sort of girl who didn't need a reason to get upset, small things were enough to irritate her. I tried to call her to pacify her. She was constantly ignoring my calls and finally I received a message from her.

'See the moon with the pole star! Quick.'

I went out to look at the sky and called her but she ignored my call. She had this habit of texting me about the thing she might be doing or enjoying even when she was angry with me. I thought of messaging her.

The moon is you and the star is me,
The moon is angry but the star is gloomy.
The moon looks cute but the star looked fused.
The moon is comely and the star is ugly,
The star is arriving from above and far,
Just to say how adorable you are.
Don't be angry you charming beauty,

The star loves you a lot my Priety.

She immediately called and said.

"I hate you. But I loved the lines. We can meet when you get back. And I would be eating your head all the way to Goa. Love you. You are my soul mate." She said happily.

No wonder how pathetic my poem was she always liked it and often that would bring her down to a stable loving mode. And on the day of journey she was excited as if she was going to Goa, constantly asking me to call her and let her know about each and everything. Don't get off at every station, be careful and use your phone carefully. She kept on messaging.

Pune:

A loud whistle brought me back.

"Please board the bus."

The conductor asked all the passengers standing at the stand to get into the bus. The bus from Pune to Goa was about to leave and I was frequently checking my cell to see if there was a message from her instructing me, advising me, shouting at me as it was two years ago. I was reading all the messages she had SMSed me that day as I had retained them all. I thought of answering them thinking that I might again get a reply from her but was invalid thought. I got into the bus and noticed the young couple.

"Bring me that water bottle. Have you kept the bag there? Why are you stupid? Keep my bag there. No I want chips."

The way the girl in the front seat was talking to the boy and the loving way in which he was responding to her it seemed that she was as dominating, sensitive and cute like Priety. The boy seemed as obedient, caring and idiotic like me. I was trying to ignore them but was silently enjoying their small little fights, pranks they played on each other, their naughty whispering that I couldn't hear but felt. Finally, she just put her head on his shoulder and he adjusted himself to make her feel comfortable so that she could sleep. I saw the boy kissing her forehead and that too mischievously and behaving as if he was just getting settled on his seat.

"You kissed me fiend?" Priety inquired skeptically raising her head from my shoulder on our way back to Jalandhar from Chandigarh during our 7th semester training in Pun-bus.

"No Priety! I was settling down and…"

"And you kissed me, you cunning monkey." She interrupted and then smiled, impishly pinching me.

She held my arm tightly with her right hand curling through my arm and her head back again on my shoulder. I wanted to kiss her once again and after looking around and making sure that nobody was looking at me I went to kiss her forehead but my cell rang and I was interrupted.

"Oh hi Yogini! What happened?" I asked.

"Hi, what's up!" She said.

Priety immediately raised her head, moving her hair falling on forehead sideways, squinted at me grimacing as if she would kill me. For a moment I was left blank with eyes wide, mouth open and lips fluttering to explain something to her that I couldn't I can't.

I cut the call abruptly telling Yogini that I would call her later as I was on the way.

Yogini was just my training batch mate and a good friend, but once to tease Priety I had said that she had proposed to me. I never knew yogini would call right at the time when I was going to have the cutest moment in my life kissing my love and showing all the respect I had for her.

She didn't utter a single word but asked for my cell and started to explore the inbox. Priety herself talked to guys, made friends, got proposals but never ever allowed me to interfere in her life as she felt that one should give space to one's relationship, though she never allowed me even to inquire about anyone as she herself told me everything when she was in a good mood. But when it came to my friendship with other girls she would probe and doubt me.

Promptly she managed to extract Yogini's number from the dialed list and called her and said.

"Are you Yogini? You better stay…… "

She could say only that much when I immediately snatched the cell and cut the call.

"What did you do Priety? She is training with me? What would she think of me? We are together in same project. She is assisting me." I shouted.

"You idiot! You call her now and say her that you have a girlfriend and she is in Chandigarh." She instructed.

"But who is my girl friend? Are you my girl friend?" I inquired.

"I don't know but just tell her a lie." She boldly stated.

"No I can't." I said.

"Oh I got it; that means you don't love me and are interested in her." She responded

"Are you crazy? She is just like a friend to me. And what do you mean I don't love you. How many times would I keep on proving it to you." I argued.

"I don't know anything. If you love me then do what I say." She commanded and turned her face towards the window. She never ever admitted that she was my girl friend and she hated this word and always believed that we were the best of the friends and always said that I should not go anywhere till the point she get married or we both.

Did I look like an idiot? Did I look like a fool? I would go and make girlfriends. But I never did, instead I always had to agree with her. What a weird girl she was!

We were crossing the dam on the way to Nawashehar. I could see the water flowing under the bridge, the birds flying around the flowing water, the green grass and wild plants nearby. For half an hour she constantly looked out of the window and I kept on trying to catch her eye. When she got angry it was really hard to convince her, if I tried to talk further I knew she might raise her voice to the pitch that the whole bus would think that I was teasing her and Priety would be the first one to kick me.

So we remained quiet for almost one and a half hours and then when we were about to reach I tried once again to talk to her but in vain. The only option I was left with was to call Yogini and tell her about the virtual girlfriend I had in Chandigarh.

"Hi yogini!" I called and said softly.

"Hi, finally you reached home." She asked.

"Ya I want to tell you that I have a girlfriend and she is in Chandigarh." I stated.

"So why are you telling me suddenly? What happened to you." She inquired.

"Nothing I love sharing my secrets with everyone." I said and disconnected.

Priety was staring at me constantly and she smiled.

"How sweet, you are my best friend. You fight with me which you can always avoid. Now I will get down from bus, don't call me as I would be with my parents. Bye love you." She said happily and went away.

Back in 2009:

I don't know when I dozed off thinking of her and when I got up I was at Panjim in Goa. I took the bus from Panjim to Vasco and then to Nofra and finally got down at the naval base station near Goa airport. I remember all the roads as I had been there earlier so I reached my maasi's place at about 9 am in the morning. I collected the keys from their neighbour as my uncle and maasi had left for their respective work.

In the evening I woke up with the door bell and found my uncle and maasi at the door. I was expecting a tough session with uncle as I remember the last time we had spoken on phone when I had rejected the offer of a job in the army and my uncle had banged the phone down in anger. I had always been under fire as if I have been a refugee serving under him. On the contrary my maasi like my mother would always support and take my side directly or indirectly. But to my surprise I found a different side to uncle this time.

I touched their feet and greeted them. I was literally in fear of being thrashed and was trying to not to make direct eye contact with my uncle.

"So how are you my son? Hope you had a safe journey? Let me freshen up and then we would talk. La la la...Hmmm hmmm." Uncle stated and went singing his own composition.

I was shell shocked and stared at my maasi with eyes wide open.

At the dinner table I had a chat with uncle and our conversation took a sudden turn to the spiritual discussions, life after death and God.

"I don't think there is anyone who listens to us." I said affirmatively.

"I don't expect this from you. You used to believe in God and went to a temple everyday. What about that?" Uncle asked.

"I used to but now I don't, I think I was immature and impractical. May be that's why." I said.

"So you think that the people who believe in god are immature and impractical." Uncle said softly.

"Maybe they are or they try to pacify themselves and believe that everything that happens is just God's will to satisfy themselves only when they are left with no options. If there is a God then why we fail and lose things we actually don't want to in life." I said aggressively. Uncle didn't say anything but quickly changed the topic. I was also wondering why I had got so impulsive. It's just that when one loses someone so close he starts pointing fingers at the one he trusted so long. In my case I held God responsible for everything.

The next day my uncle took me to a place where he believed his life had taken a great turn. I was reluctant to go but out of respect I just couldn't say no to him.

It seemed like a meditation centre and I could see the board with an image of powerful light. It said in bold letters '*Supreme Godfather is bringing the world of peace and Happiness for you*'.

Everything inside the room was red. I could see a few people sitting with their eyes closed and in deep meditation. The ambience was so pure and perfect that caste a magical effect on my mind. I sat there with uncle and noticed him closing his eyes and going into the meditation mode. Seeing him I also closed my eyes to meditate. But I could only feel the restlessness in my mind that was running with thousands of unusual thoughts. Then as in a flash I saw my last seven years. Priety, time spent with her , the ways in which I had tried to attain her, the losses I suffered in my small business, the prayers, the cries and the last good bye to her and abruptly I opened my eyes, could feel the pain in my heart and my eyes filled with tears. There were many questions in my mind and I wanted somebody to answer them. Looking here and there in desperation my eyes located something just at the left side of the wall near me. It was a chart showing a chat with the God.

God: Are you free?

Me: No! Who are you?

God: This is God. I heard you crying and thought I would talk to you.

Me: I am busy now and have lost faith in you.

God: What are you busy with?

Me: Don't know but I can't find time to pray to you anymore and I don't feel like. I am deeply pained.

God: I wanted to give you some clarity and resolve your doubts.

Me: Tell me, why has life become a hell now?

God: Stop examining life. That is it has become a hell.

Me: Why am I constantly unhappy?

God: Stop expecting anything; just concentrate on your work. You tend to expect results which you are not supposed to. You are worrying because you are expecting, it has become your habit. That is why you are not happy.

Me: But how can I stop worrying when I have so much unpredictability?

God: Unpredictability is certain, but worrying is optional.

Me: But then, there is so much pain because of unpredictability.

God: Pain is certain, but suffering is optional.

Me: Why am I suffering?

God: A diamond cannot be polished without friction. Gold cannot be purified without fire. Good people go through difficult situations, but don't suffer. With that experience their life becomes better not bitter.

Me: how should I cope up with tough times?

God: Always count your blessings, not what you are missing. In short count your positives and learn from the negatives.

Me: Sometimes I ask why it happened to me. I can't get the answer.

God: When you suffer you ask, "why me?" When you prosper, you never ask "Why me". Life is not what you plan but what I plan and I have the best for you.

Me: How can I get the best out of life?

God: Face your past without regret. Handle your present with confidence. Prepare for the future without fear.

Me: Sometimes I feel my prayers are not answered.

God: Again you are expecting and there are no unanswered prayers. Sometimes the answer is NO.

I wondered as to whether what happened was planned or destined. I closed my eyes and with full faith I tried to meditate. I found a little peace this time. For the next two days I kept going there with my uncle and finally on 20th night I boarded bus back to Pune.

FLAT

I came back from Goa and Simer came to take me along with him to Kalewari Fata. On reaching the flat I met two other guys who were living there with Varun. I was introduced to Puneet who was working with another great MNC, A BCA guy who had been in Pune for the last one year and was Varun's schoolmate. He was from Ludhiana, a bit plump but smart with tremendous communication skills that could sway anyone.

"Hi this is Puneet. You must be tired, take some rest and then we will go swimming." Removing his ear phones, he greeted me.

He put his ear phones back and went out as he didn't want to disturb me or may be he didn't want to get complaints from his sweetheart that he had ignored her for a new guy in the flat.

I was reminded of the days when Priety and I were always on the phone after college or during college breaks or public holidays, or personal holidays or almost each day since the 12th standard. She would be sharing the activities of the day with me and that too with so much enthusiasm that always made me wonder how energetic a girl could be and I had to be on my toes to respond to her as she might ask me what she had been discussing.

Her daily routine was very cute, her fights with her friends, the compliments she used to get that always made me green-eyed etc. etc. I would feel like killing those idiots who dared even to look at my sweetheart. And that was not enough! Her daily routine from the moment she got up in the morning to her shopping, buying new ear rings, new dresses, moving to the relatives coming to her sweet house, swinging from them to a delicious dinner where hardly any dish was prepared by her as she never knew how to cook and finally to our loving chat in bed.

I loved her being so talkative and her impatience when it came to listening to me. Oh God I was missing her when I saw Puneet going out with his white ear phones hanging and saying 'no no my bachu! I am here only and always be with you'.

"Come, this would be your room and he would be the guy sharing room with you." Simer introduced me to Vikas. Vikas was an MCA guy serving in our MNC for the last two years. He was a typical

Punjabi guy, of heavy built, a bit aggressive in his way of talking, using all the helping verbs that are obviously censored and that too in a single sentence. But he was a nice guy who was the sole earner in his family supporting his mother and sister. He was a bit different from the others, one for whom everything was pragmatic.

Simer went to another room and I had good chat with Vikas. He gave me some valuable tips on how to survive in the company and how to handle exams though he himself had flunked many times. Like a typical Punjabi guy with don't give a damn attitude he was guiding me.

"What if I didn't clear the exam?" I asked concluding our conversation.

Oh phen di**** ....parwa nahi.....f****.......ho jayga clear. Get lost sal****. Vikas said and went to the balcony for a cigarette.

After filtering the sentence I was able to gain confidence and could figure out that I would be able to survive in the company.

At 8 o clock we got together for dinner. Varun and Puneet took us to the nearby Mata ji mess for dinner.

Varun: hey Puneet! Should we tell them the condition to live in our flat?

Puneet: Ya man! I think they should know so that we could be relieved.

Me: Condition? What condition?

Simer: Oh men! Now don't say that we have to clean the utensils or washrooms.

Vikas: No….no guys. You just have to play hide and seek.

Me: Hide and seek!

Varun: It's just that the owner had given this flat for only three people but we are five. So it's a risk, if he saw us together he would throw us out.

So the condition was that we would all live in that flat but would not go out together so that the landlord does not know how many of us are there. Simer and I were not allowed to move out during day time and if we had to we would be careful and at our own risk. If at all the landlord came to the flat, Simer and I would hide where we wouldn't be caught. Both of us had to accept the offer as we found that the reasonable share of each more than compensated the inconvenience. Even Simer suggested the same condition and to adjust two or three more guys as it would reduce the rent to just a few bucks. How stupid the suggestion was to make our living place a poultry farm.

So finally the first official day as an employee came and Simer and I took a cab from our flat to the office. We were in on time as I checked on my watch, it was 9.30 am. But to our surprise no body was outside as we moved near the room and were able to see everyone sitting and paying attention to the person giving lecture pointing towards presentation.

"Sir may we come in. We seek for the permission."

"I guess you are late guys." The Trainer replied.

"Sir its 9.30 am." I replied humbly looking at the watch on my left wrist.

"Somebody please make an effort to let these guys know the exact time." The trainer asked the class.

"Its 10 o clock." The whole batch shouted tittering at us.

Simer looked at me with his eyes wide open and said

"Pehle din late kara dita. Saleya Ghari wich nawa cell pa." (You made me late on first day, kindly put new cell in your watch)

We apologized innocently and we were in.

It was the first lecture of C and Data structure. The very first day we got the date of the first exam. It was in a week's time. So we were all anxious and asked the trainer how we could clear the exam.

"Relax guys! You are all engineers and you are getting worried as if you are taking an exam for the first time. It wouldn't be difficult and you can all make it." The trainer replied consoling us.

But before we could relax the HR head Mr. Chirag came to greet all of us.

Good morning all of you. I guess by now all of you have got flats or PG-accommodation at convenient locations. Yaa....ya(a slang used by him after every sentence) So I am here to discuss a few policies and the exam. We are particular about the timings and I request this batch to come on time everyday. If you come after 9.30 you would be standing out and enjoying the lecture there only.... yaaa...ya.

Simer stared at me and I tried to ignore and concentrate hard on what he was saying.

"And prepare best for the exam as this would really be like a tough nut to crack. If you guys score even half a percent less than 70 it would be a golden handshake."

Golden Handshake! Everybody was surprised with this term. I thought it might be some form of reward. But he himself cleared it when he said.

"It means an exit from the company. Yaa ..ya."

Oh god! The trainer just said that we can clear the exam easily and this HR is contradicting his statement.

Who asked him to go and scare the newcomers till they started to sweat. Every time he arrives, he gives us some shattering news. As if some higher authority has given him an incentive to make us all shiver.

Finally at lunch we all came out to relax a bit.

"Yar I couldn't find a single piece." Simer said in a pitiful voice.

"Piece! What piece?" I asked.

"I mean a girl that I could stare at. The whole country is inside the class but not even a single girl that could sooth my eyes. I thought I would make a girl friend after college as everybody said first study hard and get placed somewhere, then you would be a free bird." Simer lamented.

I couldn't say anything instead I smiled and nodded. A good friend is one who would support his friend at any cost no matter how stupid his thoughts are.

Even I needed to find my love all over again. So the search for both began there.

She winked her eyes while tying her loose straightened hair, she was wearing a fine red top with denim jeans and I was stunned.

"What a beauty! Her eyes seem to be like Priety." I said suddenly while having lunch with a spoon full of rice in my right hand staring at the girl sitting at the next table.

"What!" Simer inquired turning back following my eyes to the girl I was gazing at.

"Wow! Both are beautiful." Simer exclaimed.

For a moment I was really trying hard to look into her eyes. Something in them turned me on. I was lost. She was sitting where I could easily notice her, constantly chatting with her friend. Lunch was over and she got up to leave. We finished our lunch to follow them but I didn't know where she got out from. Even in the session after lunch I was thinking of her. Her eyes were exactly like those of Priety. I was excited.

The day was over and we reached our rooms trying to hide ourselves from the watchman, the nearby shopkeeper, neighbours, each and every guy who was near our flat thinking that they might tell the owner. Though nobody suspected us but when you know you are doing something fishy you always think that everyone is watching you. Once in we would now move out only in the morning and our remaining friends were to bring us dinner every night.

Simer was really fond of English movies dubbed in Punjabi and he often made everyone laugh by using the dialogues in our daily conversation. He made us all see Spiderman dubbed in Punjabi. It was quite amazing that the Hollywood film maker spends crores to make a movie and there are great artists who work on them further to dub it and make it sound atrocious. For the first time I saw a such film and I still remember how we were laughing so loudly that we got a warning when the watchman asked us to keep our voice low but we switched lights and went to bed only when Varun got a call from the owner.

The next day at lunch I was thinking of the same eyes that had taken me by surprise the previous day. Who was she? What was her name? How could I talk to her? I was discussing all this with Simer.

"You are worried about your girl? What about me? I am still looking for one." Simer giggled.

We were standing in the queue for our veg combo meal. I don't know where Simer went in between as I turned back and was stunned. The same girl with those magical eyes was standing in place of Simer. I was again trying to look deeply into her eyes. For a moment she tried to ignore me by looking the other way, but finally she said.

"Please move forward."

I turned back and took a few steps. What should I ask her? How should I begin? Gaining self assurance I turned back and asked her.

"Are you from BPO?" I stuttered.

"No No I am from technologies only." She firmly replied.

It was a matter of pride for guys or girls in technologies as they could explain about them in length to prove that they were not at all from BPO. Believe it or not my question actually worked as she explained everything in a flash.

"I am working in that project and I sit in building-2. I have been in this company for the last one year." She added quickly.

"I have just joined. This is my second day. You must have gone through the same process and exams a year back." I asked innocently.

"Yes! The exam criteria are for all. You have to clear them to survive." She said.

"Can you please provide us with helping notes?" I asked.

"Yes sure! My friend has all the notes with her."

She introduced me to her friend Priya Singh. Finally Simer came and four of us lunch had together. We could not talk much as we were concentrating more on the food or maybe we were a bit inhibited. As we were about to leave she said.

"It was nice to meet you. Give me your number so that I can call you when I get the notes by tomorrow." She asked softly.

I passed on my number happily and was constantly thinking about her resemblance to Priety especially where the eyes were concerned.

"Hey! By the way, you didn't tell me your name." I asked abruptly.

"Palak!" She said softly, waved and went out.

"We were moving quietly to our flats stealthily as usual. And then

"Hey boys! Would you please tell me about the 2 BHK flats anywhere for four or five people?" A strange voice inquired.

Though we did not have a clue but when it comes to giving free advice and assisting others, no one can compete with us.

"Yes uncle! You can get flats in this building." Simer replied confidently.

"And you can get it at a cheaper rate." He added.

"But I guess he won't be able to get for 4 or 5 people, that would only be for three people." I added.

"No my friend is also new here. Uncle don't worry, you can easily get what you are looking for. The owners here are very cunning. They won't allow you more than 3 people but you can keep more as everyone here does." Simer advised.

The stranger left and I glared at Simer.

"So what! He seemed to be a nice guy. We should help him." Simer covered up trying to pacify me.

We slept after watching few English movies dubbed in Punjabi. Early next morning the bell ranged. No one was awake. I got up and saw Simer half asleep moving towards the door with his hair loose.

"No no no Simer! Don't open the door." I shouted.

But before I could run and stop him he had opened the door.

"*Hanji daso*!" Simer asked rubbing his eyes.

"Hi I am the owner and I am here to collect the rent." The man replied.

"Oh please come in." Simer replied, came back to his bed and covered himself with the blanket and went back to sleep.

The owner inspected both the rooms; I could see him counting again and again on his fingers the number of guys in the flat. By then everyone had got up, trying to hide here and there.

"Oh no! He is the same guy who was inquiring about the flats yesterday." I whispered to Simer.

Simer then was now wide awake and afraid.

"*Aho yar! Ih main ki kita*" (oh no! what have I done?) He whispered, trembling.

I guess Simer had not tied his turban so the owner didn't recognize him.

Owner: "So there are five of you living here."

Varun: "No sir we are three."

Owner: "Do I look like an idiot? I can see all five now."

Puneet: "No sir he is our cook (pointing at Simer)."

Simer: "Yes sir, I am cook."

Vikas: "He is my cousin and would leave by this weekend (pointing at me)."

I nodded and the owner kept on staring at us for a few minutes and then asked Varun to give him the rent. Everybody went inside their rooms and came out.

Puneet and Vikas handed Varun their ATM cards with the pin number on pieces of paper. I was standing quietly as I was not supposed to pay anything.

"Here is Rs 2000, my share." Simer proudly handed the money to Varun.

"Oh shit! Phen*** what the f***. Stop him." Vikas whispered in my ears

If he is your cook why he is paying?" The owner asked.

"I am surprised that the tenants have empty pockets and the cook has cash." The owner said sarcastically and asked Varun to come with him. Varun arrived after 15 minutes shouting and asking for Simer but Simer was missing.

"The owner has asked me to leave the flat by Friday evening, where the hell is Simer? I will kill him." Varun shouted.

"So you are from Punjab!" Palak asked smilingly.

"Yes! I am from Jalandhar. You are from Lucknow, I guess." I said.

"It seems you have all the details about me. You know where I live, where I sit and what time I come here." She said.

No it's not like that, you told me many things about you and as far as our lunch time is concerned it is just a coincidence that I meet you every day."

She smiled raising her eyebrows and continued with her lunch.

Actually I had got all the important information about her from Varun as he was in the same building and at the same bay with her. If Simer and I were released for lunch earlier we would always wait for Palak to arrive and then we would just join them pretending as if we were there by chance and not by plan. By then we knew when they would come for lunch so we were the ones who always started to ask the trainer for a break the minute the clock struck 1. Looking at us the whole batch started to feel hungry and trainer would always be left with no option but let us out. As far as Simer was concerned he could fit in anywhere and enjoy any company but the one who always used to feel bored or ignored was Priya as Palak used to grab all my attention. Sometimes I even forgot to say hi to her.

Talking to Palak was amazing as time used to pass like anything. She had her own style of talking, dressing and the most amazing was the way she used to laugh.

Priety used to laugh so loudly that even guys sitting miles away jumped up from their seats wondering from which corner the laughter that had hit them, was coming from. Her laughter was so natural, not like the typical girlish giggle. I used to love that and keep on making her laugh by cracking jokes, imitating people around and she used to laugh a lot when I imitated her. No doubt I always made faces and kept looking here and there whenever Priety used to burst into laughter as people nearby always used to give me a dirty look as if I had committed a crime. If ever I asked her to lower her volume she immediately reacted with her eyes wide open lowering her voice kept her hand on her mouth and look here and there and then to everybody's surprise she would burst out laughing all over again.

I was trying to find the same quality in Palak but; something was missing.

"Hey do come tomorrow! I will bring something for you." Palak said excitedly.

"What?" I asked.

"Surpriiiiiiseeee!" She said excitedly, waved at me and left earlier that day.

"Oh! I love surprises." Simer whispered mischievously when I told him about it.

The next day I waited the whole day for her, only Priya turned up for lunch. As usual Priya and I hardly conversed as most of the times I would ask about Palak she would end up saying just one line and that's all. I guess she was getting bored but Simer made every effort to amuse her with his jokes and one liner comments. Palak was on leave that day, I was wondering if that was the surprise she had talked about. Taking leave and leaving me constantly thinking about the Surpriiiiiiseeee. How unusual!

By 7 o clock we were all in our flats. The bell rang and as usual Simer went again to open it. I don't know why he always opens the door so promptly expecting a bouquet from some girl or expecting that a girl would come up and ask him for a date.

"Hanji dasooo….! Oh Teri….. Namaste uncle…….. How are you?" Simer stuttered.

"So guys I guess you all are ready to leave by now." The owner shouted.

Oh shit! How could we all forget that we were supposed to leave the flat by today. I don't know how it slipped from our minds.

"Uncle please sit down, dinner is ready. I made it as I am the cook. "Simer tried to pacify him."

"Oye he will get us all screwed. Please stop him." Vikas whispered angrily.

Things seemed to be well under control and we might have got one more day to shift but Puneet suddenly shouted at the owner.

What was wrong with Puneet? Why was he shouting? We could have asked day politely for one more. I whispered to Varun.

He had a fight with his girlfriend, maybe he is just upset! Varun replied.

The argument heated up and finally we had to intervene to pacify both the parties.

"Leave this flat right now or else I will call the cops." The owner shouted angrily.

"Cops! Why?" I said.

"Cops! …*yaani…pulicee…..Kyoooo?* Simer asked.

We then ran here and there to pack our things quickly, the towel hanging on the chair, the jeans on the hook on the door, the bed sheets, oops! Our wet undergarments hanging on the windows, the TV set, the tube of toothpaste even the toilet soap … we briskly packed them all. Everything was jumbled up and within fifteen minutes we ran out. Puneet and the landlord were still shouting at each other.

"Don't worry guys." Puneet assured us taking his mobile out of his pocket.

He then quickly dialled some number. He spoke for few minutes on his mobile and asked us to follow him to the nearby flats at Nisarg B Phase1. Fortunately the owner of that building was there and with his help we got a nice 2 BHK right then as one of the families had vacated it the day before. We came to know later that we were the only bachelors staying there in that building and before handing us the keys the owner warned against any complaints against us.

SURPRISSEEEEE AND SHOCK

The weekend passed quickly. I was excited to meet Palak, waiting eagerly for the surprise she had talked about last Thursday. A sweet wave from Palak brought a smile to my face as I saw her coming with Priya in a yellow suit. She was looking different on that day; her face was glowing more as if she had been awarded a fairness cream reward.

Surpriiiiiiseeee! She showed her right hand and kept on smiling and gave me sweets.

"I didn't get you. I said softly putting half of the sweet in my mouth."

"Idiot you didn't notice my ring. I got engaaaaged! Wow Na!." she excitedly expressed.

"How! .....I mean wow! ....Yes! .....congrats! What a beautiful surprise." I said covering my shock.

April 2009:

I was given the man of the match award when my cricket team won in Jalandhar in April I came back and was resting when I got a call from Priety.

"Hey Priety! How are you dear?" I said.

"Hey I won the match today and it was awesome. I know you don't like me talking about my matches but still I would like to because I won it." I added.

She remained quiet, finally broke the silence and said,

"I got engaged .The guy is nice, earning handsomely and has a family business as well."

I was absolutely stunned. I was running short of words and did not know what to say.

"Are you happy?" I asked controlling myself.

"My family is happy." She responded.

"Congratulations!" I could say only this and she disconnected the call.

Back in flat:

How can a girl be so excited after her engagement! What a big thing is it for them. Just be normal! I said angrily to Simer in our new flat.

"Oh veer! Leave that now. Why are you getting serious?" Simer replied.

"I am not serious but it is unfair. I mean not again. I mean ......" I said perplexed.

"What do you mean not again? '*Life is like a keyboard so always have an escape button to run out.*" Simer said.

"What? What do you mean?" I said looking awkwardly at Simer.

He always talks like that; I don't know how he comes out with such one liners. You can't resist a smile or digressing from the main topic.

"Right from day one I was not in favour of Palak. Have you ever noticed Priya, she looks stunning and I think she is better for you." Simer replied.

"What do you mean by saying Priya is better. She is ..... She talks ....." I paused thinking hard about her.

"Yes's...... she is better? ... She is better.... Her smile is like Priety's....her style....oh I might fall in love once again." I said with a smile.

"Who Priety? What once again? What are you saying man!" Simer inquired.

"Leave it. Let us go for a walk now. This seems to be a nice area." Simer added.

I know why he was always ready to roam around the streets as he and Puneet used to follow a girl living nearby. Puneet constantly talked to his girl on his earphones as Simer trying his level best to get the attention from the girl in the locality. They had even named that local girl *Mohalle wali*. They used to spend hours following the unknown girl till the point they came to know that she home safely.

I was reading something, lying on the mattress. Suddenly Puneet came and threw himself at me.

"Oh man! I will die. Please get off." I said in pain.

"Oh no, you won't. Happy birthday man!" He wished me.

Their plan was to put a blanket on me and give me my birthday kicks and bumps. Unfortunately when Vikas switched off the light Simer again made a blunder by putting the blanket on Puneet. So I got a solid beating but Puneet got too. Varun had brought a cake and my birthday was celebrated wonderfully.

I was expecting a call from Priety as she and I were in the habit of wishing each other right at 12 or sometimes a few minutes earlier to avoid any jams in the network. But that night her call was missing.

Chandigarh 2008:

I remember last year Priety was in Chandigarh at her relatives place and I was instructed strictly to celebrate my birthday with her. So I had to leave early in the morning from Jalandhar and reached

Chandigarh half an hour late as per the time set by Priety.

"Why are you always late? Why the hell can't you get ready on time?" She shouted.

"It's my birthday today. I think we can fight tomorrow." I said politely.

She greeted me and we planned to go first to Fun Republic.

"It's your birthday so I am going to lead the way. I am going to guide you the whole day; you just don't have to worry. I hope everything is fine." She instructed.

"You always say that I can't go from one place to another or I don't know whether to take an auto or bus. But I will prove you wrong this time. Follow me." She instructed me further.

"Auto! auto! stop!" With her efforts she managed to stop an auto.

"*Bhaiya 17 sector jana hai? Chaloge.*" She asked softly.

"*Memsaab galat direction hai. Dusri taraf se milega*"(oh madam! It's a wrong direction, kindly try the other side). The auto driver replied.

"*To mod lo bhaiya.*"(*just turn around this direction*). she retorted.

The auto driver went away, looking angry. I felt like laughing.

"Why are you smiling? Can't you just let me know that we were on the wrong side?" She said.

"I guess you were to lead so you should know." I said.

"Oh you are challenging me. Now wait till I show you." She vexed.

When had I challenged her? I had just said what she just asked me to say. Finally I knew that I was to do everything she asked me to do but never forget to give credit to her. So we reached Fun Republic but could not get movie tickets. So we decided to sit in a nearby restaurant.

"I am scared that my relatives might spot me here." She said apprehensively.

This was always her pet dialogue. Wherever I took her she was always scared of being noticed by them as if they were everywhere around the corner.

We had a great time there and finally went to Sukhna Lake at 3pm. It was nice sitting on the edges watching the lake. She never remained quiet, talking constantly about anything as she always had enough to share with me. All I used to do was just stare at her tenderly, watching her adjust her hair sideways and move her eyes quickly here and there in between the conversation.

We were standing in the backyard downstairs near the Golf Course when I held her hand.

"What are you doing? "Priety asked gently.

"Nothing sweetheart!" I said drawing her closer.

"Somebody would see us. Leave my hand." She said.

"No, where's my birthday gift?" I asked her mischievously putting my hand near her waist and drawing her closer.

"What gift! I have already given you one." She smiled and whispered softly.

We kept looking into each other's eyes and then the gentle moment removed the gap between our lips to transport us to some other world. We then hugged each other and she just wrapped herself in my arms.

Pune:

I was about to sleep checking my cell for the last time as Vikas turned the lights off and wished me again and covered himself with his blanket. It was 1.30 am when my cell rang and it was Priety who wished me.

"Happy birthday! I am sorry I got late as I was busy........."

"It's ok. I understand. Thanks for wishing me." I interrupted.

A few minutes of silence and then she rang off saying that her fiancé was calling.

It's just that sometimes new relationships create a barrier between older ones. The word fiancé weighed all the loving years I had spent with her. I don't know when I finally dozed off but it was a tough night.

This was the last day before we could appear for our first exam in the company on 1st October. Palak handed me her notes and this time my focus was on Priya. I greeted her like never before giving her chocolates and thanking her for the notes. She looked stunning in her glasses and smiled and accepted the chocolates gracefully.

Palak was shocked but I didn't care. She was engaged and Simer was there to handle her. The whole conversation during the lunch circulated round Priya and her interests. I wanted her to talk more, talk anything, talk everything and just watching the ravishing smile on her cute face that reminded me of Priety.

Simer and I were concentrating hard to study at night but may be the recession year had simply taken all our skills to study as we used to during our college or school days.

"Damn! I am not getting this." I said angrily throwing the study material aside.

"Oh pai! Padna Te painna hai! Nahi te fail ho jayenga!" (you have to study else you will fail) Simer advised me.

After college I had never thought I would have to take exams again even while working! "Oh no!" I said

I remembered all my exams since the 12ᵗʰ standard Priety had always been there to study with me. She had been the topper of her class but she was always very nervous before the exam. She would be worrying and constantly calling me to tell me how much she had prepared and how much was still left which she would not be able to cover and she would surely fail. On the contrary like a true engineer I was in the habit of studying at the eleventh hour. She would call at 1am then at 2am then at 3am and so on till 5am asking me to wake her up or just be awake with her so that she could study. And I had to be at her service. I never ever feared about failing in my exams as I always concentrated more on the chapters to be left out and then glancing at the syllabus. The impact of Priety's fear was such that even in the morning prayers I had to pray to God to make her pass. Maybe God wondered and said,

"Oh my child! Better worry about your own exam. She would top and you would be preparing for the same examination again."

Both of us forgot to put the alarm on as we dozed off while studying, maybe just half an hour after opening the study material. Simer kicked me and woke me up shouting. Now we were a bit scared, we started to move quickly and got ready. We always left after having our milk, so Simer kept the milk for boiling along the Vikas who had already kept his on the gas.

"Oh man! Why have you put so much sugar in the milk? Are you mad?" I shouted at Simer.

"Why is this milk tasteless? I put sugar in that. Oh man!" Vikas shouted at the same time.

I guess Simer understood the blunder he had made by putting

sugar again in Vikas's milk and forgetting about his own. So he disappeared.

Both of us came out with glum faces as we had flunked the first exam. But later on we gained confidence knowing that only few had passed.

"Hey Priya is coming." Simmer nudged me pointing at her.

"Don't let her know that we have failed." I instructed him and started to move towards canteen.

"But where are you going?" Simer asked.

"To get chocolate for her!" I replied.

"You have failed to clear the exam! Concentrate on your exam first. Give her chocolates the next time." He said.

"Oh exam will come again and again but I might not find love the next time." I said and left.

"Hey Priya! How are you?" I greeted her smiling and gave her chocolates.

"Chocolates! Again, I guess you have failed." She said while taking the chocolates from me.

"Better take sympathy from her by failing rather than fake appreciation of passing." Simer whispered as I looked deflated.

"What sympathy?" I shouted.

He took me aside and said that he had told her how I had studied the whole night wrapped up three books and notes but still failed.

At lunch Priya consoled me, citing the examples of all the people who had failed first and then cleared the very next time and now were at top positions. But I was searching the same Priety smile in her.

"You know what! karwa chauth is coming and I am very happy?" She said excitedly in between the conversation.

"What karwa chauth and why you are happy?" I asked at once, surprised.

"Aarekh promised me that he would give me a diamond necklace on karwa chauth." She said smilingly.

"Who is Aarekh?" I asked with eyes wide open.

"He is my boyfriend and we have loved each other since eighth standard." She said.

"You are committed! But why… I mean…. That's great….. And so sweet of him!" I said perplexed.

Return all my chocolates. And please stop smiling like an idiot. I couldn't say that; rather I waited for the lunch time to get over.

"How can two idiots be committed since 8th standard?" I exclaimed.

*"Aaho pai! Oh Te bas aiwe hi….*its just like an old saying." Simer said.

"What old saying?" I asked.

"Like …..Like….nothing…. I was not in favour of Priya. Have you ever noticed that we have failed in our exam and have just a day left to prepare and clear it this time? You can fall in love after that. You *pacharkhau!*" Simer covered up.

We had no option left but to study and study hard. We gave our best this time and finally we cleared our exam. So our first round in the company was clear and the next exam was slated after about fifty days.

We had ample time left to study. Varun bought a cake with 'FIRST EXAM CLEARED' written in bold on it and we celebrated by cutting it.

"May I come in?" I asked the new women trainer gently. She had been appointed for the corporate training programme.

"Oh come in." she said.

The class was looking different this time as I noticed many new faces staring at me. For a moment I thought I had come to the wrong class but then I saw Simer and my group just sitting in the third row smiling at me. The new batch from Mumbai was supposed to join us for the corporate training directly resulting in adding strength to our batch. The trainer was fair lady with short golden hair and impressively well dressed in her black corporate suit. I was bit nervous as the new trainer seemed to be bit rigorous. Before I could snick through her fierce look and get myself seated she asked me abruptly.

"By the way dear why are you so late?"

I never expected such question from her as I thought that it was her first day but I forgot that I was no longer a college student coming late for the first lecture. I was running short of reply and taking away my bag from my shoulders I gave her the most innocent look I could.

"Corn… flakes…were ….na….not ready. He gave…… me….a…. late and I got late." I bumbled.

The whole class started to laugh as if I had cracked the biggest joke of the century. It was a fact that I had stated. I could not figure out why they had burst into laughter.

Raising her right hand and making the whole class quiet, she took a few steps towards me and raising her eyebrows in surprise she asked,

"What? What were not ready?"

"My breakfast in the canteen was not ready." I said

"Oh your breakfast! You could have left that. You had a class and you knew it." She said.

"No…. Actually I paid… fo..o..or …corn flakes." I faltered again.

She could not stop herself from smiling this time and asked me to introduce myself and warned me never to be late in her class.

"Why didn't you wake me up?" I whispered exasperatedly to Simer.

"I tried but you were lost in your dreams. I guess you found love there as well." He giggled.

"Shut up!" I whispered angrily.

For a few minutes we concentrated on the lecture being delivered by the new trainer. But I don't know where Simer was focusing. Suddenly he found the source of distraction and exclaimed in surprise.

F-e-u-t-i-b-u-l....

"What?" I asked.

"I mean beautiful. Look at her. She is so cute." Simer stated.

Feautibul was a dialogue from Simer's favorite Punjabi dubbed movies. I guess after exploring the new batch he found few beauties that he could go out with.

I looked in the direction he was pointing at it. The girl was actually very cute. She had let her hair loose as it still wet. Hair falling from the left side covered the left side of her face. I found her tucking her hair behind her ear. The eyes with *kajal* were concentrating hard on the trainer's lecture. Her glossy lips were parted and her face was as fair as the full moon she reminded me of Priety. She was just five seats away from me on my left. Her exquisite blue suit with the floral designs was adding charm to her beauty. How serious she seemed to be in the lecture as if it was the most interesting one.

Priety used to attend lectures like this. I always used to wonder how one could write everything delivered in the class as well as work on various other things too. Like reading novels, making notes of other lectures or texting messages to me. On the other hand I used to perform only one task and that was to reply her. She always wanted me to reply quickly to her messages but I couldn't expect the same from her. If I was in a mood to talk to her she would sometimes feel the boring lectures to be significant and completely brush aside my messages but her puckish temper sometimes made her ignore even her most important lecture seeking a reply from my side. She kept on throwing messages constantly if I delayed in replying to her getting emotional, aggressive or sweet texting and asking about ignoring her.

Once she wanted to go to a movie and she messaged me.

"Hey! We would go for a movie." Be ready.

She never had to ask anything from me, an order was enough.

"Movie! Why movie?" I replied keeping an eye on the teacher delivering the lecture.

"What do you mean why movie? You don't care about my plans. I wanted to spend some good time with you and what a cold reply from you." She regretted.

And that took me completely out of the important lecture I was attending. After all who would give an importance to the lecture when a gorgeous girl wants to spend some time with you.

"No, I mean which movie? I wrongly wrote why movie. How can I ignore a movie with my love?" I replied covering up the deliberate mistake I had made.

After waiting for ten long minutes I thought of messaging her again as she never took so much time to reply. She was sure to be angry so I had to write something soothing to make her smile.

"Priety baby! Are you there?" I asked getting romantic.

Still no reply from her. I started sending messages again and again quoting few romantic lines, a few songs and finally after forty minutes of completely wasting my lecture I got a call from her.

"Are you insane? I was attending the lecture and couldn't reply. Don't you understand the simple things? You never allow me to attend the lecture. I won't go for a movie with you. Go to hell." She said aggressively and disconnected the call.

What rubbish? Who messaged and asked to go for a movie? Your lecture is important and mine is of no value. What about the times when you keep on messaging me? I said to myself as even I knew that I couldn't ask her. I had to pacify her first.

"Where are you boy?" The trainer shouted and brought me back to the corporate training session. I apologized and she didn't complain much. Throughout the three hours of the lecture I kept on looking towards my left trying to get a good view of the cute new girl.

Fortunately, after lunch the same girl sat with our group and we came to know that she was not from the Mumbai batch. She had already done half of the training in March 2009 and due to health problems she couldn't complete. So, as per the company policy she was supposed to complete the training with our batch.

"Wonderful policy! Great man! Did you hear that?" I said to Simer as we both tried hard to overhear the conversation that she was having with members our group as we sat in the row behind her.

"I am sure you will find love this time as I have found mine. Look at the girl in pink." Simer said pointing at the girl sitting in the fifth row.

"What about your *mohalle wali then?*" I asked.

"I will choose the best one." Simer giggled and we both laughed.

The next day I reached five minutes early and managed to sit next to her. By then she had got to know our group rather well except for Simer and me. As usual I was nervous about starting conversation with her. She was wearing a light green suit with cute little stars shining in the gold ear rings she had on. Simer nudged me again and again asking to say 'hi' to her at least. I tried hard many times but the words just wouldn't come.

"What are you doing?" I shouted, punching Simer as he pinched me thrice gesturing to me to ask her name.

"You are just sitting and staring at her. Talk to her, say something." Simer said.

"I don't know what to say to her." I whispered.

"Say something to her. She doesn't know that we know everything about her." Simer said.

"Hi! Its such an interesting lecture Na!" I said abruptly cutting off

Simer and turning towards her.

"Ya these corporate lectures are always interactive." She replied cutely.

"What's your name? I guess you are from Mumbai College Na!" I asked innocently pretending to know nothing about her.

"Shradha!" She answered.

"Wow! What a name?" I said to myself and smiled.

"Why are you smiling?" She asked.

"No…no…Nothing…." I faltered.

"And I am not from Mumbai College. I have already completed half of my training and …… ………."

She kept on saying various other things but I was concentrating on her cute smiling face and her head nodding again and again. For a moment I was lost thinking about just me and her alone in some romantic place with me kneeling and saying a few cute lines about her beauty. She was so cute that one couldn't say it in words. How quick I was thinking in just a flash and forgetting that I hardly knew her.

"Hello! Hello! I have finished." She pushed me bringing me back to her conversation.

I was smiling till the point I noticed a red mark on her forehead. A dot that took all my attention and I could not resist asking her about it.

"Hey what's that red mark high on forehead?" I said smilingly.

"Its *sindoor*. For my loving husband as every Indian woman for hers. You know it is part of Indian culture. She said smilingly.

At once my smile faded. With a stunned expression I looked at her.

"Are you sure… You are married… I mean. How? Actually…. when?" I stammered.

"What? What did you say?" She inquired smiling.

"Yes I mean, are you sure that you are married? I mean you don't look like a married person." I sounded confused.

She just could not control herself and said laughing,

"Yes I am married and even I don't feel like that sometimes. See you after lunch. She waved and went quickly to join my group.

For a moment I felt lost as every dream with her seemed to be shattered with a small red dot. As if somebody has given me a tight slap when I was kneeling down and saying a few sweet lines to her about her prettiness. What an irony! Why can't girls remain single till they find someone nice like me? You don't miss an achievement award if you get married late.

THE SIZZLING RAINY ENCOUNTER

"All beautiful girls are either engaged or committed or married damn it." I said getting furious and looking at Simer back in our flat.

"Yes!" Simer said.

"It seems that the companies are recruiting girls only on condition that they should not be single." I said again

"Yes!" Simer said.

If half of them are married and the other half engaged what about me? Where would I find my love? I said sounding angry.

"Yes! Yes!" Simer said again.

"What yes! I am serious." I kicked Simer and shouted.

"*Ha pai. Ki kara main*!" Simer stood up sounding frustrated." I have also lost my *mohalle wali*. I saw her on a bike with her monkey today while coming back to our flat."

"Oye…sal****. There are other better things that you can do and think of rather than finding love everyday." Vikas commented. We both stared at him in rage as if he has asked us to leave the flat. But we didn't oppose, of course who would want to have a nasty blow from that heavy built chap.

"Why do you guys want to get committed? Stay single boys! Life can be enjoyed better when you are single rather than when you are engaged." Puneet added smilingly.

"And there is no fun! …….. Oh shit! Ritu calling." Puneet ran hurriedly to answer the call.

"Sorry! Sorry! my love …I forgot …to …call you." Puneet sounded apologetic and his voice got lower as he went out.

"Look who is advising you. Another fool hanging around the corner!" Vikas stated and went out for his cigarette session.

I went to the balcony to get my clothes which were dry by now and saw Vikas smoking. He always seemed to be very serious while smoking. As if he was not smoking, but burning his heart out. The pain of missing something could very well be noticed on his face and every time he would check his cell while smoking looking more and more bitter. Muttering something he would keep his cell aside as if never ever to pick it up in life.

"Why don't you quit smoking?" I asked gently.

"I tried but now I don't want to." He said curtly.

"It seems that you miss someone!"

He turned, stared smiled and then concentrated on his cigarette.

"Oh come on! You can share your feelings with me. Maybe that could puff out the real smoke that's eating you up."

He finished, threw out the stub and then said,

"I just loved her like I might not be able to love anyone in future. We were together for so many years. The day I proposed to her, the days I dated her, the days we laughed, we cried, we spent together, to the day I saw her for the last time were all like a dream to me. A dream that I would love to have every night, a dream that never stopped and a dream that could be substituted with the rest of my life; it is merely a dream now. And that dream is no more a part of my life now.

Vikas was mourning his lost love and I could see a replica of my life in it. I could well understand his state of mind. The agony, the pain, the curse and the void he had to deal with. For a moment I went silent.

"Why did she leave you?" I asked him, placing my hand on his shoulder.

"She did not only leave me but left this world forever. It's really hard to be at the funeral of the one with whom you thought of spending your life." He said and went inside picking his cell up from the balcony.

I was in a state of shock thinking of the brutality of life he what was facing. It was a day when I felt that my pain was nothing in front of Vikas had experienced. On one hand I was no doubt missing someone special with whom I had shared many dreams and on the other I was thanking God and asking for my love's long and happy life even if I could not share it with her. It's sometimes difficult to be in someone else shoes. How fortunate you consider yourself when you notice that someone else is facing harder problems than you.

It was again one of the sleepless nights I was contending with. Till the point I did not know about Palak, Priya and Shradha's being engaged, committed and married, there was hope of finding love but now the same virtual feeling was not there to wrap the torment of missing the golden days spent with Priety. The weather was bad that day and it seemed that even the clouds were covering up the sky bringing all the emotions they had and were releasing them to solace. Lying on my back I could hear the raindrops falling sharply and could feel a cool breeze through the open window. It could have been a romantic night on any other odd day but it's just the human emotions combined with his perception that could view the same thing in a different mode in accordance with his state of affairs. Inside my heart was shedding the drops and I recalled the romantic rainy days and nights of my past.

2007:

"It's raining outside. Go and check out." Priety messaged me way back on a July afternoon in 2007 during our training days in Chandigarh.

I could very well imagine her feelings and expression of enjoying the falling drops from heaven. But I didn't answer her; it's just that you enjoyed sometimes teasing your loving girl by not replying at the moment she wanted you to do so.

"I am missing you. Where are you my 'lover boy'?" She messaged again.

Lover boy was the romantic compliment given to me and that too from her favorite actress Julia Robert's movie. In fact Lover boy was the only valid romantic name other than words like monkey, dog, fiend, idiot and joker she had coined for me in response to the romantic words like angel, sweetheart, doll, pari, gorgeous, beautiful, exquisite and so on coined by me. How incomparable and different they seemed to be when you put them up on paper but in fact they were the ways we used to express love and our respective feelings for each other.

I couldn't resist this time and answered her. It is the obvious effect of the girl on a boy in so much deep admiration that he can't ignore her for long.

"I am here only my love enjoying the rain with you."

"You stupid, can't you see that I want to talk to you. Call now." She replied.

I was getting ready for the birthday party thrown by my friend in 17 sector and I was already getting late. But still I couldn't resist calling her and resulting in building my enticement falling in coherence with her temptation to talk to me in such an amorous weather.

"Hello my lover boy!" She whispered after picking up my call.

"I am missing you soooooooo much." She added excitedly in the same murmuring voice.

That was enough to strike down the stupid birthday party and spend some great time on call with her.

"I wish we could be together in this lovely weather. I said hoping against hope.

Ya I too wish the same. She said in her excited voice.

But you live far from me. Why didn't you take PG near mine? She added raising her voice.

I was staying at sector-20 in Chandigarh and she was residing at Mohali phase-9 with her relatives. That was hardly 20 minutes distance on bike at pace but even that seemed to be so far in excitement of love.

"Oh your lover boy is so curious to be with you. I am coming." I said abruptly.

I didn't even think that it had been raining for the past two hours and it would not be possible to reach her place easily and on time through the enormous traffic jams but that is so called the power of love that can make you think of doing and going crazy without giving a second thought. No doubt she tried to stop me from coming but I know that was just a formal attempt by her. Even she was getting curious to see me.

Fortunately the heavy rain turned into the light drizzling and I was happy that even rain God is with me and favoring the true love I had for her. It's just that you feel so good sometime when such coincidences happen and gets added with your blind desires. I took my bike out, kicked it thrice and paced up to the desired destination. The journey in the rain was quiet smooth with my mind occupied by thoughts of seeing her till the point I heard the horrible noises of vehicles almost struck to each other in the traffic near sector 34. Well! That was on the cards. I was prepared for that so I took extra 20 minutes from Priety to reach there. But just my luck, the traffic didn't move an inch even after 15 minutes of wait. I was getting impatient as I was constantly receiving her messages full of excitement to meet me. I tried hard to zip in between the cars and autos but all in vain. Finally after a long wait the traffic moved a bit, I just reached 35 sector markets but only to find that my bike would not move. I was already in the middle of traffic and could not find space even to get down and check the damn trouble with the bike. Just then I got a call from her.

"Hello! Hi Priety. I am just on the way and about to reach." I said calming my nerves.

"Oh my baby! pleaz come fast." She said romantically.

"Coming Priety!" I said and cut the call after saying bye.

Suddenly the light drizzle changed to heavy rain again and the noise of horns increased. I could see passers by running to find shelter, some people standing under the trees and trying to cover their heads with their handbags, files or polythene bags. I was left with no option to park my bike there at 35 sector parking and wait for the rain to stop. I had got completely drenched by then.

Oh no! This stupid rain spoilt everything. Everything seemed to be irritating at that point of time and even the rain god was not being spared by the thoughts full of anguish and complaint running in my mind.

After a short spell of the heavy rain became a light drizzle. I decided to move from there to take an auto. But the traffic was so sluggish that I was left with no option but to walk briskly. I got so tired after reaching petrol pump near sector 40, I checked cell and was astonished to find the calls from her that I hadn't picked up. I didn't know how but while walking I hadn't felt the cell vibrating.

"Hey Priety! You called." I said breathing normally after calling her.

"Where are you now? It's been an hour. You said that you would reach in 40 minutes. You always lie." She fired.

"And why were you not picking up the call?" She added fiercely.

There is such a traffic jam that I ..... and my bike.....and...Hello...helloo?" I could say that much before she disconnected angrily.

Priety was always peculiar about the timings. If I said forty then it had to be forty minutes only, not even a single second here and there. It was not her concern that there was traffic jam. For her everything was moving well so I should also be. I just checked her message after a few minutes stating.

"No need to come now. Go back and rest. Take care."

What the hell was this? I had been struggling since the last hour trying to make my way through this traffic, the ugly smoke, the irritating noises, and the turbulent rain just to go back and rest. Why couldn't she understand my state? I thought of messaging her same but instead I opted to run. My marathon ended near 44 sec circle from where I took an auto till phase-9 Mohali. The traffic was clear by then and I was now late by one and half hours.

I reached the cricket stadium near phase-9 and called her. Obviously she didn't take the call. I messaged her about my arrival but she didn't respond. She had warned me secretly to not to even pass by her relatives place as if they might get suspicious about her. They hardly know about me and my face but still it was Priety's fear so I had to obey her. It was 7 pm by my watch and after waiting half an hour for her I gathered confidence to move forward till her relative's place which was behind the cricket stadium. I reached there and gave her a call again but this time a ray of hope aroused as she cut the call instead of letting her cell ringing breathlessly. I went passed by her house ignorant as if I am new to that place and searching something. I saw a man outside the gate near her house may be it was her maternal uncle enjoying the weather with his dog wetting the pole outside.

I called her again and she didn't pick again so I messaged her scene that I was gazing at outside her gate. In a span of five minutes I took four rounds of the same place, and every time I pass near her gate my eyes automatically turned towards the balcony at first floor as she was staying there only.

What are you for son? Uncle asked at the gate and with his dog now constantly searching something by poking his nose as if somebody has planted a bomb there.

I was stunned at once started to shiver thinking that might her uncle had pierced my intentions of meeting her niece inside.

"Nothing …..a…I ….am…new searching for an….address."

Which address? Tell me the house number. He stated boldly.

By then his dog finished his search and even had stopped wagging his tail and started to stare at me as if he had found a terrorist who planted the bomb he was searching a while ago.

"Actually uncle…i..i..just..forgot..the address….but no worries I will find…….Oh no!" I could say that much only that I saw Priety standing above at the balcony.

"Oh no!! Oh no!! I mean I am getting late. Th…thanks uncle." I stated covering up the shock and ran to get out of site.

I had hardly taken few steps the cell rang and it was Priety's call. I knew I would be on fire. So I thought of ignoring the call but I picked.

"I warned you to not to come near my house. I don't know what my uncle would be thinking of me?" She fired at me.

I didn't utter a single word, kept on listening to her, because I knew if I said anything she would ring off, so I kept quiet and waited for her to finish all she had to say, she stopped against me after five minutes of firing.

"Where the hell are you?" You fiend! She asked.

I didn't say anything. Actually I was feeling low and sorry for myself. I wanted to retaliate but knew I couldn't with her. By that time she realized that she had been harsh and a bit unfair too. So she spoke to me in a slightly lower voice me, still riding her high horse.

"Are you there? Now speak up please. And I am sorry." She said.

Her apology did the trick, it charged me again. Now I knew she would listen to me. So I said each and every thing to her about how

I had managed to reach there and was feeling bit cold. She understood how I was feeling. There was silence when I finished.

"Now I don't want to meet you Priety. I am going back." I said, getting emotional.

"Shut up! You fool! What do you think of yourself? Stay there and I am coming in five minutes. Don't dare to leave. I will kill you." She ordered.

Who would now dare to leave? I stood there waiting for her and thinking about how sometimes being emotional worked on her. I could see her coming towards me walking briskly, wearing a ravishing white top with dark blue jeans.

She came closer and without greeting asked me to follow her. She took me to nearby market and then she stopped at once near the ice cream parlor.

"I am sorry. I always get angry with you. But you always do things that spoil my mood." She said.

"I am sorry Priety. I don't know how I got late and …."

"Now just be quiet and let's sit here only as I need to leave in 15 minutes. It's very late." She interrupted.

I ordered her favorite vanilla with hot chocolate sauce. She loved chocolate sauce so a cup full of chocolate sauce covering each and every tip of vanilla was specially ordered for the lady in white. I was watching her behaving like a kid and so excited that she could hardly wait to put the spoon full in her mouth. How quickly she forgot everything and was enjoying, laughing and continuously talking as she always had a lot to share? To my surprise she filled the spoon and quickly moved it towards my mouth and ordered me with her shining eyes to have some.

"You are lucky my lover boy. I don't share my favorite ice cream with anyone." She stated teasing me.

I was smiling and her presence made me forgot each and every difficulty I had faced in the last few hours to reach her. Those fifteen minutes with my angel was like finding a gold coin in the dust.

"Oh shit! I am late. They might come here." She exclaimed in shock after checking the time on her mobile.

She stood up and was about to leave when I held her hand.

"*mat jao!* Please don't go. Stay with me for few minutes na." I said tenderly.

I could see her getting calm and staring at me with those lovely eyes full of love.

"I want to be with you my lover boy. But I have to be home by now as they would get suspicious. We will meet tomorrow for sure. Now get up you monkey." She whispered.

I quickly looked around me, then drew her close to me and closing my eyes I kissed her.

She removed her hand from mine abruptly, she punched me twice and threw the water in the glass at me and moved out quickly laughing mischievously. I left her near the cricket stadium and left for 35 sector to pick up my bike.

I came home at 10 fully drenched after getting my bike repaired as it was raining again. I was so tired that I went to bed quickly after changing. She called at 12 when I was asleep.

"Hey! Lover boy. Are you awake?" she whispered.

"Ya...ya Priety I am." I said rubbing my eyes.

Whenever she used to call me at night I always tried to appear as fresh as I could, trying my best to show her that I was fully awake. She was in the habit of asking the same question 'Are you awake?'

"I am missing you dear". She said in her soft voice.

Oh that moved me. I was completely awake by then. How good do you feel in bed talking your love in whispers with lights switched off, wrapping yourself with the bed sheet, feeling as if the one you are talking to is lying just next to you. Her voice seemed to be different, with falling drops outside adding more spice and sensation to the moment.

"I am missing you too." I whispered.

"I always hurt you. I am a bad girl. I am sorry for everything." She averred softly.

Priety always used to feel very guilty after yelling at me. She wouldn't admit it at once but after a few hours or a few days she would herself start to apologize for what she had said to me. She would keep on apologizing till I said something romantic or at least paid her a compliment.

"Don't be sorry Priety. I love you the way you are. My sweetheart is not at all a bad girl. She is the precious diamond that God has gifted me." I whispered closing my eyes and then kissing her over the phone.

She smiled and kissed me back. How crazy people in love sometimes turn out to be. The phone tends to receive all the passionate kisses that one throws and the same kisses flowing through the network, crossing all the signals and creating a link between the two.

"I wish I could spend more time with you." I said.

"Even I wanted the same." She added.

"I wish I could come to your place." I said getting more romantic.

"At this time! Are you crazy?" She said.

"By the way what will you do after coming here?" She asked further.

"First you have to assist me to get in. Alright." I said.

"Alright my loverboy! Aajao." she said and laughed.

"First I would climb the wall and then take the stairs till I find your room." I said.

"What will I do?" She asked innocently.

"Obviously you will open the door and let me in."

"Then I will close the door….and …" I could only say that much.

"I will run to call uncle." She added mischievously, interrupting.

"Stop it Priety!"

"Oh shooolly my lover boy! Continue." She stated.

"Then I would stare at you in your beautiful pink night gown, and you would throw pillow at me, then I would come close to you."

"I will then ask you to sing for me." she added immediately.

"What? Song? Which one?"

"I don't know you have to sing for me and impress me." She said like a princess.

"Alright, I will then sing and it would be…. *Main koi aisa geet gaun , ke aarzuu jagaun , agar tum kaho….*"

Singing the line I would ask you to reach out a hand kneeling down and you would stretch out and I will continue "*ke tumko bulao, ke palke bichau kadam tum jahan , jahan rakho, zameen ko aasmaan banau, sitaron pe sajau…..*" then I would dance with you holding your waist with your right hand in my left one. "*agar tum kaho….main koi aisa geet gaun ke aarzuu jagau*".

"You would lift the heavy shadow of your lashes and look at me with your beautiful eyes."

"Then I will keep my hand on your mouth." She joined whispering softly.

"Then I will pick your slender body up in my arms and keep you suspended in the air with my eyes gazing yours." I responded.

"Then?" She asked softly.

"For a moment you will struggle but then you will give up to the feel of the moment completely melting in my arms. My hand will touch your slim throat and feel the pulse beating there like a captured sparrow. Your glistening lips will be near my mouth and ……"

"And then…." she whispered and I could feel her breathing hard.

"Then I would take your name in a low tremulous voice and so will you and then ……." I paused to listen her breath and then continued.

"And Then I would close your flowerlike mouth with one long kiss."

After few minutes of dead silence she whispered.

"Run! Run!"

"What Priety?" I whispered getting amazed.

"My uncle knocking" she said sounding scared.

"Uncle, at this point of time…. Is he a watchman?" I sound angry.

"Shut up! I will call you…wait…." She said and rang off.

I was wondering about the stupid uncle spoiling the romantic encounter, but what a tremendous feeling that was.

PRIETY, RIYA AND THEIR CONFUSIONS

"I will talk to her today. I have to and I will." Simer confidently stated pumping his fist.

"To whom will you talk? Your *mohalle wali*?" I giggled.

"Shut up! My *pink wali!, my pinki!, my sweety pie!.*" Simer replied.

"But what will I talk and how will I start?" Simer asked.

I started looking here and there trying to ignore him feeling amused. Simer came forward and kicked me hard.

"I am asking you. You will help me now. Tell me how to start the conversation." Simer ordered.

I turned towards him, controlling my smile. I thought of helping him to and find his love.

Priety always got angry with me during my college days when I helped boys in impressing their girlfriends. She would yell at me and tried to warn me to stay away from other peoples lives. I used to wonder what was wrong in helping others. No doubt I was always successful in resolving fights, in the process making a mess of my love life. I tried a lot to hide it from her but she was far too sharp. She would always get everything out of me by sweet talking and once I let out everything she would simply make me sit on a frying pan.

"What about Disha's case? Is she fine now with Rohan whom you helped?" Priety asked softly.

"Who is Disha? I don't talk to them, it's their personal matter." I said trying to sound nonchalant.

"How was your day Priety?" I asked trying to change the topic.

"Please don't change the topic. I came to know from others. Why can't you tell me? Why do you hide things from me? I won't kill you." She pleaded with me.

"There is nothing Priety, I am not hiding anything." I said again.

"Then why didn't you turn up when I asked you to see me in the evening. Even your cell was busy. Now don't lie. Please Na!" Priety said complaining.

"You don't trust me and you don't love me now. You neglect me for others. Oh Cummon you can tell me."

"Yes Priety, they....they ...... are both .... Happy now." Finally! I said expecting a tongue lashing from her.

"So you helped her again?" She asked but to my surprise very cutely.

"y....y..yessss..... I had to help her." I said.

"Great my lover boy! You are their hero. In fact you are a love guru. I am proud of you." She said sounding excited.

"Oh Priety! Are you serious?" I asked.

"Yes of course. Do you think I am that rude?" She said smilingly.

"Oh hoooo Priety. I am happy now. Actually even Ashish is going through a similar phase. I will help him too. You know it is so good to see the patch up between them. You know Disha was praising me and she said................"

I said and blurted out everything. She kept on listening for the next ten minutes.

"Oh shoo cute! What a wonderful person you are!" She exclaimed.

Then the storm burst. "I have not seen such an insane guy like you. Why don't you understand that they just use you?" She said raising her voice.

For few seconds I couldn't make out whether she was praising me or cursing me but very soon the messages was loud and clear *"Beta tu to gaya!"*

"Damn, you think that you are their love guru. You are a fool. How many times have I asked you not to poke your nose in affairs of other people? But you don't realize this. You hardly care for me. You are .... get lost." She blasted and cut the call.

Pune:

"Oh man! She is coming. Where the hell are you?" Simer shouted and punched me.

"Oouch..Idiot! Here only yar." I said getting irritated.

"Shall I go now and what should I say?" Simer asked me.

"Wait! Wait! Be patient. We will talk to her after lunch. Till then you just keep on observing her." I said.

"What do you mean? Only I will talk to her. You'd better stay out." Simer said and smiled.

Simer and I were late again after lunch. I don't know when Simer went two steps ahead of me and he opened the door when I was still busy in waving to Palak and Priya. But to my surprise when I turned to open the door I found the lady trainer with the whole batch staring at me with Simer standing by my side looking stunned. Before we could seek her permission to enter the room she said,

"Hope you have finished waving to the girls? Or do you need more time to say good bye? We are ready to wait till then. You can go and escort them to their respective floors"

"I ... i...am ....ss.....sorry ma'am." I faltered.

"All right come in. But let me know why you are late this time." She asked after letting enter.

"We got our meal late." I offered a lame excuse.

"Yes, there was a long queue at the veg combo. Simer added.

Trainer: What? How many of you had the veg combo today?"

Half of the class raised their hands controlling their laugh.

Trainer: See, they managed to come earlier.

I: Actually ....they...they... were all in front of us.

Trainer: Very good! So whad did you have in the veg combo?

By then the trainer knew that we were not lying but not telling the whole truth. But she turned the conversation in such a way that what could have been nasty for us turned light. The trainer asked us questions and our answers became more and more stupid.

Me: Rice with chana.

Simer: And with *tulsi ka patta* on it.

Trainer: what? what? Tulsi???

Me: He means tulsi leaves on it.

Trainer: Ok leave that. Tell me about *tulsi ka patta*.

Me: It's a plant that we all worship and it's grown in Jalandhar.

Simer: And in Amritsar also.

Trainer: No, where is it grown?

Simer: In *gamlas*.

She could not control herself and burst into laughter asking us to occupy our seats. "Don't be late next time." she warned us.

We sat on our respective seats as we were paired alphabetically. Simer was sitting in one corner of the class. I got his message.

"Why the hell didn't you allow me to talk to Pinky? You didn't want to as you seemed interested in her. I hope you are not searching your love in her"

I read and turned to look at him; he looked very angry and I smiled at him. I didn't allow Simer to talk to her for the whole break. He constantly kept one eye on the table where his *Pinky* oh I mean his girl was sitting.

The session got over and we came out at 4 pm for our tea break. The two of us stood holding our cups and Simer was complaining again.

"Ok, I asked you to look at her. What did you see?" I questioned him.

"Ya, I observed her purple top, her smiling face and blue bag." Simer stated confidently.

"Did you observe that she is wearing a purple band to tie her hair after loosening them seven times the whole day? Did you observe that she writes with her left hand? Did you notice the dimple on her right cheek? Did you hear her when she introduced herself during the act?" I said.

"No… No…. Why the hell did you notice all this?" Simer said.

"Oh! Idiot, I did it for you only." I replied.

"Ok, but I still doubt you." Simer said raising his eyebrows.

"All right, do keep all these points in mind. Now go and talk to her, compliment her about her performance but don't let her know how poor she was while acting. Initiate a basic conversation and for God's sake let her speak more about herself." I ordered.

"I won't go alone as her friend is with her, so you handle her friend." Simer said getting nervous.

"Hey, you performed rather well there." Simer complimented her, sipping from his cup.

"Thanks!! I enjoyed yours as well. You seemed to be a nice actor." She replied smiling.

"Ya thank you. Even I used to perform during college and I played Shahrukh's character and ……" Simer started again.

I gave him an ugly look with eyes wide open, asked him to shut up and ask about her.

"And I performed in youth festivals… nice blue bag you have, with purple clip you have a nice dimple when you smile ….tell about yourself. What is your name?" Simer covered up and blurted out.

"Pardon? What did you say?" She inquired.

"He means, you are carrying a nice combination, I mean it's nice, and we couldn't hear your name." I intervened.

"Yes… yes….your name" Simer added getting confident.

"I am Sonal." She introduced herself and put her hand forward.

Simer punched me hard on my back when I shook hands with her and introduced myself.

"We both know that you guys are quite popular." She smiled and commented sarcastically.

"And she is my friend Riya." Sonal added.

"Hello!" Riya said and they both laughed and went to keep their cups inside.

"What rubbish? Why did you shake hands with her?" Simer asked.

"Why did you blurt out everything? I asked you to keep something about yourself from her and let it out later while talking to her and not at the beginning." I lashed out.

"Now, what should I do? " He asked.

"First get to know her and then flirt, you fool." I said.

We were so busy making our plan that we didn't notice when both the girls came and interrupted.

"Shall we go for a walk?" Sonal asked.

"A…aa ya ya …Sure. We have 10 more minutes before the next session begins." I stated abruptly faltering apprehensive that she might have heard us.

Simer nodded with his eyes widened, compressing his tongue

between his teeth and turned his back at once when he saw her asking for a walk.

He was quick learner and seemed to be happy while talking to her every time he found time during the small breaks we used to get in between the lectures. He broke all the rules of flirting as he did it wildly and sometimes making her feel how weird he was, but that's what he was. But there was another story that was piling up on the cards and that was mine and Riya's. I had to be with Riya so that Simer could have good time with Sonal.

Riya was from Mumbai, but to my surprise she never ever seemed to be from the city of dreams. She seemed to be an introvert, family oriented and diffident. It was really tough to get things out of her. While talking she would just talk to the point and that's it. But she had stunning looks that could even divert the attention even of a guy with poor eyesight. I sometimes wondered how her beauty simply compensated for the boring company she could be for someone. She would hardly laugh even at the jokes that I cracked, there were situations where I started to doubt if I had lost all the wit and humour I had been proud of.

The corporate training days were passing quickly. It was the last day the whole batch would be together as after that it was supposed to be divided into two groups leaving the Mumbai batch that joined later. Simer was as usual flirting with Sonal but hardly saying anything that she might be impressd by.

"Which is your favourite colour?" Simer asked Sonal.

"I like pink." She replied.

"Oh mera wi, I mean mine also." Simer replied with a smile.

"Pink is pink and pink is everywhere in my mind in my heart." Simer's one liner was meant to impress her.

"Waise, I don't love pink now, I like red." she said without paying much attention to his comment.

"Same here red, roses are red, your sandal is red, please don't change the colour else I would be dead." Simer giggled.

"What?" She inquired smiling.

"Here is a flower for you." Simer plucked a flower from the plant behind him.

"This is yellow, I know you like yellow also." Simer added.

Riya and I laughed when we saw him doing all he could to impress her. The more he tried to flirt with her the more she played with him. Simer was running here and there those days, trying to look for the beautiful rhymes he could from the Google, he would arrive at office looking like a Zombie the first two days he didn't even change his pink turban confident that pink was her favourite color.

"Excuse me! I will be back in a moment." Riya went to her phone.

The break was over and we went back to class. The lecture started and still there was no sign of Riya. I was curious as to what happened to her. I asked Sonal about her but she said casually that she would be somewhere around. It was not the first time that she had gone out so suddenly. So I preferred to concentrate on the lecture rather than think about her. The trainer was discussing how to categorize people on the basis of their behaviour, their nature, their choices and their thinking. Depending on that people would fall into the category of the Expresser, analyzer, driver and relater. These were the various personality traits that people might have. Suddenly Simer nudged me again.

"Boss! What to do now?"

"Just drop a simple SMS to her." I ordered him.

"Ok …. but I don't have her number." Simer said innocently winking.

"Why didn't you ask her?" I asked, irritated.

"Actually I tried but she said she didn't have a cell." he said.

"Oh ho."

"How to get her number because I noticed she had a cell." He added.

"Oh she is just playing with you." I said with smile.

"Tell her that you wanted to say something to her that you heard. But you can't say it here as it is confidential and important." I said.

"Yes! Yes! But what will I say when she asks me to tell it to her." Simer asked.

"Oh that we would see later. First get her number." I said.

"No but what will I say......." Simer could only say this when he was interrupted by a loud voice.

"Both of you get up." the trainer shouted.

"What the hell are you discussing? Now both of you will discuss it with the whole class." She added.

The whole class left everything and stared at us as if we were going to say something wonderful. Many of them were pointing fingers at us and some were teasing us making fun of us.

"What now? What now? Plan? See your plan misfired again ...damn!" I yelled up at Simer.

"*Le das yar*! What did I do?" Simer looked blank.

"Didn't you get me? Discuss with the whole class. Please." The trainer shouted again.

Simer: yes madam!

Me: what yes! Are you mad?

Simer: I mean No... No madam.

Trainer: Can you guys speak a bit louder? We can't hear you. It's an important discussion, so I guess we all need to hear it. Does anyone want to miss that?

Class: Noooooooo.

Me: Nothing! We were discussing the lecture only.

Simer: Yes! We can change our personality by our behaviour, thinking and character in corporate world. The person with analyzing skills can be a good driver.

Me: No No idiot! (I whispered)

The whole class busted into laughter.

Simer: And …..And sorry maaam.

Trainer: Yes Mr. do you have anything to add what your friend was saying. (Smilingly she pointed towards me)

Me: Actually we missed the later part of the discussion.

Trainer: because you fools were busy with your own discussion.

We both apologized and the trainer finally couldn't resist herself from separating us by shifting me to the last corner seat. Things seemed to be fine now, the two negatively charged electrons were separated and the whole class was able to concentrate on the lecture. I was able to concentrate for hardly fifteen minutes after which I started to think about Riya and the reason for her absence in the class. I took my cell out and dialled her number just to find that her cell was switched off. I don't know why I thought of her in some problem and was anxious. I wanted to go out of the lecture. Thinking all the possible reasons and gaining confidence I stood up.

"What happened now?" The trainer at once stopped and asked me.

"I have a severe headache. May I leave and get some medicine?" I asked innocently.

The whole class turned back to gaze at me and after my plea a few started to smile again. I was wondering now about the damn reason that made them titter again. The trainer stared for a few seconds and then permitted me. Before I could reach the door and pull it the trainer moved towards Simer and said.

"Now I guess you also have a head ache or stomach ache."

"Yes…oh no no….. I am fine… Fine." Simer bumbled.

I came out looking for Riya but couldn't find her anywhere, I went to the canteen, searched all the towers but she was nowhere. Tired of searching I gave up, thinking that she might have left for her flat. I was going back from the library back to my lecture room when I saw a girl crying, hiding behind the tree nearby. I remembered that Riya was wearing a dark green top so I could make out that it was she who was sobbing and when I went close I was sure. She didn't notice me standing behind her. I was caught in a dilemma whether to talk to her or ignore her. I thought of choosing the second option and turned back to attend my class leaving her alone.

"No mom, please stop crying. I can't see you crying like this." She was responding to the call shedding her tears.

I abruptly turned back and was stunned. I moved few inch closer to her when I saw her ringing off in anger and throwing her cell aside. I saw her wiping her tears with her handkerchief and then she stood up and seeing her I turned again and started to flee from the place. Just then she shouted.

"What are you doing here?"

"Nothing ….nothing I was just passing and saw……." I said.

"What did you hear?" She interrupted.

"Nothing" I replied.

"Are you all right?" I asked.

"Yes I am." She smiled trying to look cheerful.

"Are you coming for the lecture?" I asked again.

"Yes I am coming. Let's go." She said and started to walk briskly.

We just took a few steps and I couldn't resist asking her why she was not attending the lecture. She just stopped walking and didn't say anything.

"I am sorry but I saw you crying and I am sorry again as I tried to over hear your conversation and………" as soon as I had said this her face crumpled and she started crying.

"Oh no! I am sorry. I didn't hear anything. Please stop crying." I said to pacify her.

By now I got nervous that she did not start to shout. People passing by might start thinking that I was teasing her and lodge a complaint against me. After a great deal of persuasions I managed to quieten her and make her feel a bit lighter. We then moved to the canteen. After glass of water she finally spoke.

"My parents are getting separated." She said.

She told me the whole story and I came to know that there was a lot of bitterness between her parents. They had realized that they were incompatible within few years of marriage. It was because of their daughter that they didn't divorce but now, things were out of control. Her mother was facing hell and wanted relief from.

"How can I see them getting separated? I lived the whole of my life together with them. I love both of them and I know they love me too." She said and started sobbing again.

There was something unusual I noticed while she was crying. I got it finally. For a moment I was lost as I was thinking of Priety again.

"Wow! She just cries like her." What a strange coincidence.

I don't know why but for a second I wanted her to cry a bit more.

You fool! Stop thinking about Priety, first console her. Help her. Listen her and advise her. I said to myself.

I tried to console her, asking her to be strong and leave for Mumbai as soon as possible. She seemed to be relieved after talking about it. I dropped her till the gate, she took an auto and went off.

Priety always seemed to be the strongest girl I ever met until I found her crying once and that too because her father hadn't allowed her to join the dance class.

"I want to join the class. Everybody does, why I can't join." She had complained.

"Yes Priety. You should join the class. So go for it." I had said.

"*papa mana kar rahe hai*" but you tell me what's wrong with it?" She said seeking for my opinion.

"Yes, what's wrong with it? Talk to him again. He will allow you." I had said holding her hand .

"Shut up!" She had raised her voice, quickly removing her hand from my grip. Everybody in the café had stared at me. I had tried to behave as if everything was fine.

"He wouldn't. He wouldn't." and she had started crying.

"Stop crying Priety." I just consoled her thinking of the actual reason that made her sob like this.

"I don't….. kn…ow ….why he behaves…..aaa … like that….. with me. "Sob.. sob.." he is rude. I hate him."

"Priety, he is your father. He loves you and what he does is only for you. You should not be angry like this." I concluded.

How cute she looked while crying! The girl who seemed to be so strong, vibrant and commanding and make the whole world follow her, the girl who just made the guys shiver when she lashed out at them was crying like a kid. And even I didn't get why she was crying.

"Why the hell are you smiling?" She immediately asked wiping her tears.

"No...No Priety. Very rude father, Very bad. He should not do like that. After all you are his lovely daughter. And you are so….so….." I could say only that much.

"So what? Why you are saying that he is rude? My father is not rude. I love him. It's just that he sometimes behave weirdly with me." She had said clearing her throat.

"Sorry Priety! But you look shoooo cute while crying. I wonder if your dad denies you things so that he can see my Priety getting more cute and childish." I had said excitedly.

She had smiled and pinched me and then continued with her coffee and grilled sandwiches.

Pune:

"So did you get her number?" I asked Simer washing utensils back in our flat.

"No, she said that she would call me. I said what you had told me but…." Simer lamented adding water while making the dough for our dinner.

"Oh morons! At least talk about your career at least once a day also." Vikas said while placing the vegetables in the basket.

Again we couldn't do anything just to stare at vikas. We had no problems in admitting that we both were bit scared of his heavy built and at most we preferred to ignore rather than being knocked down by him.

All five of us were gathered in the kitchen as every night we used to prepare our dinner together. I was supposed to wash the utensils and make chapatis. Varun and Puneet were good at cooking vegetables, Vikas in buying them as well as making paranthas and Simer did the rest of the work.

Puneet: (to Simer) Are you in love with her?

Vikas: what love? He is just fooling himself.

Varun: go and propose to her.

Vikas: *oh nahi hona is kolo*. He is scared. I bet he can't.

Puneet: Why are you scared? Always have an edge over the girl. Be a man Simer!

Varun: Look who's talking. I guess you are not a tiger in front of your girl friend.

Puneet: Oh I am not scared of her. It's just that she …she …had a strong opinion and is just a bit dominating and moreover I just love her.

Vikas: A bit dominating? She is super dominating and you are a 'joro ka gulam'.

Puneet: Get lost!

Vikas: Fuck off…...

Simer and I kept looking at each other and were wondering how we had digressed from the topic. It was not the first time that Puneet and Vikas had a spat, it was regular between the two of them. There was hardly any morning when they both woke up without shouting and abusing each other on small things.

Puneet: Oh you asshole! Get the hell out of here.....

Varun: Shut up guys!

Simer: *aaho pai , chup ho jao…dimaag kharab tuhada….dafa ho jao!* Get lost.

The impact of our conversation could very well be felt during our dinner when we all gave Simer dirty looks. Nobody could ever make blunders like him and I don't know how he could put so much salt in the dough he was making. We all shouted.

"Oh teri phen ***saley**** .just wait and I will kick your ass....."Vikas shouted.

We finished with our dinner late that night and I was standing on the balcony with Simer when I got a call from Riya.

"Hey Riya! How are you? I hope you reached home safely." I shouted at once.

"No I am on the way and would be there in half an hour." She responded.

"Actually I wanted to say thanks to you." She added.

"For what?" I asked.

"For being there with me." I am feeling embarrassed that I cried in front of you. "She said sheepishly.

"Oh its alright, it's just that sometimes we are unable to control our emotions especially those which are filled with pain."

"Yes but its just that I never expected you to be there when I actually needed someone."

"Yes it is indeed that whenever you expect someone to be with you in tough times he is never there, we always end up with someone else sometime to give us a bit of comfort." I said.

She seemed to be in a different mood at that time and I was feeling nice supporting her. For the first time I noticed a different Riya expressing her innermost feelings and sharing them with someone. Maybe she was at ease or may be she was preparing herself for the worst before she actually reached home where her parents were still at loggerheads.

"You know, even I don't have good friends who can support me. No body understands me."

"Why? I think Sonal is a good friend of yours. She seemed to be very supportive." I said, surprised.

"She is nice but still we don't get along nicely. Its just that we are completely opposites." She retorted.

"Actually no girl gets along with me, I don't know why." She added.

Her voice choked and I could noticed that she might end up shedding tears again, so I cheered her up giving all the supportive reasons I could and consoling her. I was actually wondering why she was confused as the reason for tears were her parents or her friends.

2007:

Once Priety came upset, murmuring something with her eyes brimming with tears. I was just about to ask her what had happened when she said.

"Why do all these girls create road blocks for me? Why do they bitch about me? Diya always has a problem with me, messes up my work and talks about me with her friends. Why?"

Before I could think of an answers for the questions, she answered it herself, "Its because they have a problem, I am just an innocent girl. I am weak and an easy target that can be fooled." and with every word her voice choked and before I could react tears started to roll down.

Oh God! I could only say this with my eyebrows raised and in a compassionate tone. But she retorted, "you will never understand".

"What the hell are you thinking of?" She asked.

"Nothing dear, just wondering why did she do this to you. But what did she do?

She started but it was too much of an effort to listen and somewhere on the line I switched off. She was quick to notice it.

"You are not listening to me, I feel as if I am talking to a wall". She shouted.

"No no I am....am ... listening." I nodded.

"Then tell what I said?" She asked abruptly.

I had to be an adroit to answer, as I need to recall everything and that too bit by bit so that I could convince her that I was attentive.

Finally the story was over and I consoled her saying she should be strong, and stop worrying.

"I am a strong girl and I know how to handle." She stated boldly.

Hey wait, you just said that you are weak and an easy target. What was that? Oh god! I confused. I wished someone could tell her that she was contracting herself but no one did.

She did like that now wait I will show her what I can do. Another bold statement that left me raising my eyebrows. Biting my lip I nodded.

It seems last week also I had heard the same words but poor diya still had not suffered Preity's fury? I smiled. A few minutes of silence and then she asked.

"Do you think I am wrong?"

I thought for a moment not analyzing what happened but thinking of the answer i gave last time as prooving her wrong and guilty. But then i was questioned and asked to give justification with evergreen lines 'you hardly understand , you are just dumb and you will always support other girls , because she is hot and you think that you can woo her'.

"Where are you lost again?" She pushed me.

I just nodded with my mouth open thinking of the best possible answer to please her; hey I didn't want to upset her as I cared for her. So I said that it was not her fault, hoping to appease her.

I expected a cute smile after I had finished and a cute line from her but the reaction was just the opposite.

"Why are you always biased? I don't need you to support me, just tell where i am wrong. How would I be able to correct myself?"

I said that she was not wrong but they were right too, they didn't think about her but I always had her in my mind. They might-or-might not be with her but I would always be there to hold her.

That did the trick, she was convinced now. She punched me and smiled in her cute way and said "Oh yes, I think you are right."

MY FIRST DATE WITH RIYA

I got up late after Simer kicked me hard and hollered at me. He was almost ready and had been trying for the last half an hour to wake me up as today the new trainer was supposed to come for the Java lecture. So we needed to be on time.

Simer kept on shouting at everyone and warning me again and again that he would leave me. And go to the office.

"Wait man, I'm just putting on my shoes." I said, consoling him.

Varun was also ready and the three of us left after Simer yelled at Vikas and Puneet for teasing him. Even they were surprised to see Simer so aggressive for the first time. Even on the way till we boarded the cab he went on complaining again and again. Varun remained quiet and looked at me. We kept quiet for a few minutes and then looked at each other sitting at the back of the cab. Varun and I both were hiding our smiles and finally Varun couldn't control himself and started laughing.

"Oh man! I am sorry." I said and then hugged him and seeing me Varun did the same. It was a nice moment where we three expressed our feeling for each other.

"*Acha acha bhai! Ab Sonal ka kya karna hai*? Oh what to do now?" Simer asked and then smiled.

We burst into laughter and started to make further plans so that things could work out for her and Simer.

Simer somehow managed to get her number as she called him but that was not enough, simer wanted to talk to her immediately.

Sonal was coming and Simer at once started to adjust his turban asking me how he was looking. He took the chocolate from his pocket and was about to move forward to talk to her.

"You will ignore her today." I ordered putting my cell in my pocket.

"What? No I won't. I can't." He said.

"It's ok then talk to her but don't come to me." I said smiling.

"This is not fair. I want to ….. I …."

Shut up! Don't you see that she is not paying much attention to you, so behave in the same with her." I interrupted.

She came and waved to him but Simer turned away, ignoring her controlling his temptation to talk to her and kicked the ground hard after she had passed. She was shell shocked and came back to talk to him.

"Hello Simer! How are you?" She said softly.

Simer turned towards her and was about to say something when he looked at me just to get a nasty stare from me asking him to avoid her. He did it brilliantly. Controlling his emotions, he gave her a formal smile, took out his cell and moved away pretending to make a call. Sonal must have felt terrible and she abruptly turned away to move to her class. I was about to move into my lecture room when I received a call, it was Riya.

"Hey! Where are you?" I asked.

"I am on the way to Pune, will be there by 1 o clock. How are you?" She said.

"I am fine, how's everything at home? How are your parents?" I asked.

"Well! Things are under control. I am very happy and I will tell you the rest when I am there. Be there at the gate to receive me." She laughed and rang off.

She sounded a bit different, not like the Riya I used to talk to earlier. But it was good to hear from her, so I was waiting excitedly for the lunch break to talk to her. I received a message while she was about to reach the gate, so I was there and saw her paying the fare to the auto driver. She turned and lifted her bag, adjusting her black purse sideways and then pushing away her hair from her forehead, she saw me. She smiled and waved looking prettier than ever. I greeted her, took her bag and we both walked in.

Simer saw me coming towards the canteen and came to me. He waved to Riya and then took me aside.

"You asked me to ignore my Sonal and you are having a good time with Riya. I also want to talk to Sonal. Could I go now?" Simer lamented.

"No, you will not talk to her today. Have patience! Come let's go for lunch." I said firmly.

Pulling a long he was left with no option but to join me.

Riya was constantly messaging me during the lecture and so was I. She got bored and asked me to come out with her. It was first day of the new trainer so it was easy to get the permission on the pretext of a headache. I came out and we met behind the building-2 where she was buying vada pao and a cup of tea for herself from the small canteen with special Maharashtran snacks. She offered me the same and we started to converse. She seemed to be happy and told me everything about how she had handled things at home and finally settled everything.

"Thanks again. You really supported me." She said, sipping her tea.

"Its alright. I am glad you handled things properly and now

everything is fine. Seems the big city girl has grown up." I said with a smile.

"Yes! *Yeh to hai*. I am a smart girl." She said. We went quiet and looked into each other's eyes, for a moment I thought that something happened; I immediately shifted my glance and noticed her soft right hand slightly placed on her thigh. I guess she was still staring at me.

Simer managed to ignore Sonal the next day also with his heart crying to talk to her. I got a call from Sonal asking me to tell her why Simer was behaving like that.

"I don't know may be he is upset." I said.

"Upset? For what?" She asked.

"How would I know, he is a nice guy who hardly shares anything with me these days. Seemed off color always, maybe he has lost something, whatever I don't know." I replied acting as innocently as I could.

"Why don't you talk to him? He would feel good." I added.

I told Simer about it. He could hardly control himself, desperate to talk to her. The long wait was over as she called Simer and they both went out.

Time was passing swiftly and Riya and I were getting along very well with each other. She seemed to be comfortable with me, playing pranks, sharing, messaging and bunking some of the sessions together. Most of our batchmates started to doubt that there was something between us and there were few teasing remarks too but as long as we were both clear we never bothered to pay any attention to any of that.

Riya told me about the crushes a few girls of her class had on me and flattered me, teasing me to go for this or that girl. In return I used to tease her about the senior employees who had a soft corner for her. She would smile, laugh get angry and punch me. Everyday she used to bring something in her lunch that was made in her PG for me. In return I had to give her chocolate or treat her to her special strawberry ice cream after lunch or even during the tea breaks.

I asked Riya to spend the day with me as she was free during the weekend. So we planned to meet on Saturday.

"We will go to Mumbai tomorrow." Simer asked me.

"Mumbai! Why?"

"My relatives are settled there so we will spend this weekend with them." Simer said.

"I can't come with you, as I am going out with Riya." I replied softly.

"Oh hoooooooooooooo.....Riya...Date....Great man! Finally you got love." Simer giggled.

"Shut up yar!, we are just good friends. No love shav. She is a nice girl." I pointed out.

"What's wrong with her? She is smart, feautibul and most

important she is not committed, engaged or married." Simer said smiling at me.

"Go man! She is meant for you." Varun joined in.

"No no…guys…its nothing like that….I can't…." I said.

"What's wrong with you? Are you straight or ……?" Puneet tittered.

"Just make the most of your date with her, make her day. I still remember when Ritu I and went out for the first time. I took her to FC road and see now we are just going to get married next month" Puneet added.

"*Oye eh pagal hai……tu fas jayga*…..just enjoy man! No love ….this is all shit…."Vikas advised.

"Fuck off! I am not but you are an insane pig." Puneet retaliated.

"Teri phen***…di….phen***.why did you use my soap today?" Vikas shouted.

"Stop watching my TV…..you asshole." Puneet cried.

"Oh God, they started again." Varun expressed.

"*Oye saban te TV kitho aa gaya?*" whose soap and who's TV guys? Simer shouted.

After a few minutes of fighting they all got back to their routine work and that was to prepare dinner. But they all made me think about Riya. Yes I was concentrating hard on her, the way she talked, how she laughed, her smiles, her tears, her behaviour everything about her was charming.

Now the question was to make the most of the date and just impress her. I was thinking of how to start, what to do or what not to.

Chandigarh 2007

I was late in reaching sec 35 Chandigarh. Priety had been waiting for fifteen minutes. I don't know how I got late again but was prepared to accept the verbal bombarding she would deliver. I saw her standing in her light yellow top with a floral design, she was looking hot in her goggles with loose hair and watching me coming from the parking. With a glance at her wrist watch and before I could say anything she sparked.

"Don't give any invalid reason. Why are you late?"

What can be the valid reason? How tough is that? I bit my lip, thinking hard of valid reasons but could think of nothing right then and she fired again.

"Why do you always make me wait for you? I guess you enjoy doing this, you are just….just….an irresponsible …."

"Wow! You are looking damn hot." I said hoping that my compliment might work as a fire extinguisher.

She paused, sighed, adjusted her hair and then ordered.

"You fiend! Move in. I am hungry."

I don't know how but she quietly moved in and that too smiling.

May be she would fire after lunch. It was Hotel Orange where the ambience was so good that it simply lightened her mood.

"I always order whenever we go out. You should learn to order. Girls like men leading rather than being led. So make it fast." She ordered.

I was stunned and gazed at her. Every time I went out with her she would taunt me at least once for not taking the lead. I took the menu card and went through the list but before I could think of anything and order, she stepped in again.

"I think we should order veg sizzlers, with Manchurian and spring rolls. I just love them." She snatched the menu card from me and asked the waiter to bring the same.

"What is this? I was supposed to order and lead you but instead you have already made up your mind. This is not fair." I whispered.

"What did you say? Do you want anything else?" She asked raising her eyebrows.

"No no Priety, it's perfect." I said smiling putting my elbows on the table and propping up my face.

"I will have chilly chicken also." She added.

"You should also have chicken, it's delicious. I don't know why you don't have it. Look at you, it will make you healthy. You need it." She told me.

"No I can't, you know I am a vegetarian. I can't." I said.

"I know, its ok I can't force you. I will order something veg for you." She resented.

I thought for a moment and looked at her. How cute she was looking glittering eyes, tremendous beauty, oh hoooo… I just loved her and I said.

"Alright, I will taste it today."

A guy in love can forget everything, his rules, his conscience, his nature and most of all when he gets inspired from films like '*Rehna hai tere dil mein*' scene where a Brahmin boy eats chicken to woo his girl. So did I, what's wrong with that? And how happy she was when she noticed that I was having chicken with her.

We finished with our lunch and it was great, the chicken was rather delicious. But I didn't say I had relished it so she started to feel guilty about making me have it. Seeing her I had to admit that I had enjoyed it not just the food, the restaurant, the ambience, being with her everything.

With the mood so light, with the light so dim she was on a high and asked me to order vodka.

"No No Priety! Who will take you home if you get drunk? Moreover I have never had it before." I said.

"I have also never tried before, my stupid lover boy. Just order now. We will enjoy ourselves." She said excitedly.

We had few shorts of vodka and we were giggling, cuddling, teasing each other but not that lost, pretending to be sloshed than we were. I don't know when suddenly while talking to her I held her hand tightly and stared at her with my eyes full of love for her. She also didn't try to take her hand away, instead she tilted her neck sideways, bit her lip and her brown deep innocent eyes flashed into mine. She questioned my intentions, raising her eyebrows and I just said.

"I love you."

"But I hate you." She whispered and poured drops of water on me from the glass and giggled.

Back to Pune: So I was ready for my first date with Riya. For the first time I was ready before time. She called and we decided to meet at E-Square. I left my place on time took a bus from Kalewari Fata directly to E square and was there early, I saw her coming and on an impulse I decided to hide and appear late before her. I made her wait for fifteen minutes and then called her to check her mood.

She was normal and said nothing, so I appeared before her and she gave a big smile stretching her hand forward to greet me.

"Hey Riya! I am late." I said.

"Ya I know. So what?"

"So you are not angry." I asked astonished.

"Why would I be angry dear? Its alright, everybody does get late." She replied.

"But you should be. I would love to see you angry." I said.

She laughed at once and pinched me; we then took an auto from there till FC Road. I was thinking of how Priety would have behaved in an auto, constantly chatting asking about this and that on the way and being apprehensive of being taken along a longer route by the strange autowala. But Riya was quiet, she was enjoying looking out at the moving roads through her glasses, setting her smooth silky hair beside the ear after every minute as they were blowing in the wind. I tried to involve her in a conversation, but she answered only what I was asking. I guess I was getting a bit bored but still something kept my hope alive. We reached FC Road and started to move around. We noticed many couples passing by hand in hand, enjoying each other's company.

Now Riya was talking nineteen to the dozen, invariably looking at everything and commenting on whatever came her way, asking about my views looking at the dresses of other girls, their partners and so on. I was really enjoying this, may be that's what I was waiting for; I was searching for the same Riya in her. Unlike Priety she was not walking a few steps ahead of me, she was with me.

"Do you have a girl friend?" She asked.

I paused and thought for a moment how Priety used to hate this word.

"No, never had one." I replied.

"I also never had any boyfriend. Being in a relation is just boring. Haina..." she said.

"But I loved someone." I admitted.

"Ohhhh Hoooo. Who's that lucky girl? Is she with you?" She asked curiously.

"She is now lucky because she is not with me." I tried to change the topic with a smile.

"What? Where is she now?" She asked curiously.

"She is no more part of my life as she got engaged now." I answered.

"But you can talk to her and ask why she......."

"Please Riya, change the topic, I don't want to comment on it." I said politely interrupting her.

"Oh! I am sorry. *Senti ho gaye*..It's ok. I am hungry now, let's go and have something." She said.

We went to a nearby restaurant. I remember Priety had said that girls like men leading the way. So I moved a chair for her and then sat after making her comfortable. I took the menu and was shuffling through it when Riya received a call and went for a moment to answer it. Meanwhile I remember what Priety used to order so without exploring the menu, I ordered veg sizzlers, Manchurian and spring rolls.

Riya came in a bit late and as she sat again and had a sip of water the waiter placed the order with crispy noise of hot Veg sizzler and crunchy spring rolls on the plate. She gazed at me with eyes wide opened and exclaimed.

"Oh no, I hate sizzlers. You could have waited. But spring rolls are fine."

"Can I order again? Please!" She pleaded innocently.

"Ya..ya.. Sure dear." I nodded and wondering what was wrong with sizzlers as Priety used to love them, selecting pieces of pineapples from them and put them in my mouth.

She ordered few more things and till they came we had spring rolls and Manchurian and that too she had with hundreds of complaints. But that was fine; I should not have expected her to enjoy what I had ordered.

We were finished with our meals and then she said at once.

"You know what. I love ordering myself, I never allow anyone to do so. I am very peculiar and choosy about the food I enjoy. Please don't mind."

I paused with the spoon full of gravy near my mouth staring at her with eyes wide open consciously admitting to myself that I had blundered by trying to lead her. I could very well notice that she had got bit upset initially but like Priety she didn't get angry at me or yell at me. I don't know why I wanted her to get angry with me, I wanted her to fight with me, I had made a mistake and she should make me admit that. I wanted her to get fume and stop talking to me allowing me to convince her, pacify her and give her the warmth I could but that all was in my mind.

We moved out after paying the bill. I excused myself and went somewhere and asked her to wait there only. I could feel the feeling of disappointment was still there in her. After a few minute I called her and asked her to come a few steps ahead as I was waiting there. She started to move as per my directions and after a few steps I patted her from behind.

"Here is the pink rose for the beautiful lady." I gave her the flower.

She was bit shocked to see me bringing flower for her, with a sudden change in her expressions from blue to stormy and within few seconds to a cheerful one.

"Oh wow! So shweeeet…..I just love the pink roses." She accepted it gracefully and smiled.

"Just close your eyes." I said.

"Why?"

"Surpriseeee?"

"Surprise…. as in……" She expressed and closed her eyes.

"Here is another surprise. Now you can open your eyes."

She was excited to see the small kit of chocolates and she shouted at once to thank me. That was all I was looking for, a sweet expression.

I apologized for upsetting her and she asked me not to behave formally. But I knew she wanted me to do so. She seemed enjoying herself now and she was talking rapidly and incessantly as she held my hand while walking and often she would pull me to move faster with her holding my hand tightly. I don't know why I actually did so for her but I know this was the way I used to make Priety feel great.

We went to the temple nearby and sat for a few minutes there. She was quiet as she seemed to be bit tired after roaming around and chattering. I too was tired and as I closed my eyes for a moment, I saw Priety in a fairy white dress smiling and moving far away from me, waving at me, laughing and then a message in my cell made me open my eyes. I pulled it out from my pocket and was amazed to check that it was Priety's message.

"I was thinking about you lover boy, really miss you these days. God bless you. With love

yours Priety"

Oh that message really filled my heart, hundreds of thoughts and moments spent with her darted in my mind and my eyes were on the verge of relieving the drops that were dying to come out. I was about to message her when Riya intervened.

"Hey, I guess we are getting late. Let's move now." She stood up and picked her purse.

I was brought back by Riya from the valley of sudden emotion that filled me at that time unknowingly, controlling myself I got up smiling looking at her.

We moved out and after walking few steps we reached the bus stop. She was looking here and there and abruptly pointed out at the board nearby which advertised the salsa classes to be taken by some celebrity trainer.

"Wow! I want to learn salsa." She said jumping in excitement as if she had got selected to participate in 'Nach baliye'.

How can I forget when Priety compelled me trickily to join salsa with her, throwing emotional tantrums on me, giving me all the valid advantages especially of meeting her in every class. Most of all she got attracted towards the kiss at the end of every class that she would give me? So blindly in love with zero senses and a sensual offer of a kiss after every class who the hell would reject an offer like that. I did join the class with her though I hardly got any kiss after the class but we learnt to shake our bodies with the dance beats. And at the end of every class I got hundreds of complaints about not dancing properly, sometimes about my dress, sometimes for coming late and sometimes for no reason. So I had to practice even after the class at home to impress my girl. Thinking of all that I couldn't resist telling Riya that I knew salsa as I learned it two years ago.

"Wow! You know, teach me please." She stated like an eager student who wanted to join a new class under physics professor.

"Alright, but first let's catch the bus as its 8 o clock." I said.

"No no, hey just do one step here." She said in excitement.

"What? Are you crazy?"

"Crazy as in…you know na..then please do it for me…"she said tilting her neck sideways with right index finger between her teeth and smiling like a kid asking for an ice cream.

"No I can't dance right now and that too in the middle of the road where people are already staring at me as if I am with their sister." I said briskly.

"I don't care about them. Please dance na..Please do…."

"No no no . I can't and I wont, lets go now."

"I will not go till you dance here." She said obstinately and turned abruptly sideways crossing her arms.

"*Ajeeb ladki hai*" I whispered pulling my face and thinking why I had let her know about the salsa. I paused for a few minutes and then said.

"Ok yar! But how can I do it without music?"

"No problem, I will sing." Smiling in excitement she said after turning towards me.

I raised my eyebrows with a weird look wondering how girls could be super excited about such a foolish thing like dancing in the middle of the road and that too without music. But she was.

"Hey hold my hand too." She added further.

"Why?"

"Stupiiid! You will do salsa alone." She giggled.

In such a weird situation who would want to remember anything and I was actually lost thinking how awkward it would be to dance with her singing and me twirling her round. Oh common, it was not any bollywood movie scene where a guy would be dancing with a girl and people nearly would follow taking the same steps and singing in chorus.

I looked here and there just to steal my eyes from the strange looks that came my way. I held her hand, and that moved me when I felt velvet like touch so soft, the wind blew her hair and I felt it too and that made me forget everything. My eyes paused staring at her, she was adjusting her purse and then she adjusted her hair sideways and finally she gave a look and started to sing.

"*aja piya tohe pyaar du…gori baiya tohpe waar du*"

I was instructing her to move forward and then take a step back and so on. We continued to entertain people for just few seconds when I pulled off and pointed out that it was getting late as we had missed the bus. She jumped and laughed in excitement and then I took an auto back to my place after dropping her at Vishal nagar where she was staying.

I should be happy, the day was well spent, she was nice company and I should be dreaming about her. I was thinking, dreaming and missing but not Riya. Priety's message was still on my mind and I was again in deep thought about her wondering about her sudden message and that too when I was with Riya. But that message was something significant and I know she might be upset. Having been with her I understood her more than even she understood herself. So it was obvious that she was not fine but this time I couldn't gather the confidence of calling her and asking her as I didn't want to interfere in her new life. I was really getting confused between her and Riya. Riya's thoughts should create an excitement in me, my heart beat should pace up while thinking of her but still Priety was not leaving. Even the void created by her absence was not getting filled up. On any other odd day that night would have been full of dreams about Riya and her talks but this feeling was different and instead it created a void in me.

MY SECOND DATE WITH RIYA

"Oh Priety! How come you are here in my flat?"

"Who gave you my Pune address?" I asked shocked when I found her sitting in my room in Pune.

She was wearing a light yellow long frock just like white fairy dress with hair loose and smiling at me she responded.

"Well! I can be anywhere for my lover boy."

"Oh dear! I really miss you. Please come back. I will become something soon. Just give me some more time." I pleaded.

"I know you miss me. I won't go anywhere. I am with you only." She consoled me and came close.

She just sat and I lay down with my head on her lap telling her about the company, about my exam and my friends in Pune when I heard Vikas shouting.

"Teri phen****...fuck you man! Why the hell did you open the door again?"

"You ass hole! Don't abuse. I will kill you ....damn you!" Puneet responded.

I opened my eyes just to find that I was hugging the pillow and Priety was nowhere. I got up rubbing my eyes and looked here and there and it was clear that it had been mere dream. The dejection on my face was loud and clear when I heard the spat between Puneet and Vikas again. I was wondering if they were fighting in my dreams then where was Priety. It's just that your dreams sometimes cling to the facts around you. So the fact was that they were both shouting and abusing again. Simer also got up and shouted.

"Oh pai chup ho jao...sawere sawere ki khap pai hai? Why are you shouting ass holes?"

"Stop using my iron and TV." Puneet cried.

"You fool! Stop using my laptop and soap. Just get your damn ass out of here." Vikas retaliated.

We got late again and Simer reminded me of the new trainer coming this day. Every week a new trainer was supposed to come. So we rushed to take a cab. Unfortunately we waited for about half an hour with no cab in sight. We were constantly waving out in search of a lift till Hinjewadi. A red Alto came and stopped few steps ahead of us. I ran quickly and without asking I got onto the back seat and asked the driver to wait as Simer was coming. Simer joined me and we saw the driver letting a lady enter through front door.

"Sir! Please drop us to Hinjewadi." I requested.

After giving a stern look from the mirror he nodded and started his car.

"Oye gadhe!! He is not a cab driver. He stopped for that lady and you just got in without asking." Simer whispered biting his teeth.

"Ha yar! He is well dressed and doesn't look like a cab driver. Shit yar...Is she his girlfriend?" I asked softly.

"How would I know? Now shut up and sit quietly." Simer whispered.

"What if she is his girlfriend? We got the lift and that too free." Simer giggled.

Driver: *Sho guysh! Where ju you werk?*

Proudly I told him about the company

Driver: *Sho you are new to the company!*

Simer: Yes sir.

Me: We joined this September only and we are under training.

Driver: *I guesh you guysh are late. What will you ju now?*

Simer: no problem sir! Today the new trainer is joining, so no worries.

Me: sir, tricking them is not a big deal. We are too good at that.

We both laughed and he smiled too and looked at the girl sitting next to him. She also giggled and seeing her Simer tittered a bit more.

Driver: *Sho what 'ell you shay if he ashks you?*

Simer: aa…aa… we will say that 'our roommate locked us inside by chance.'

Driver: *Whaat?*

Me: Yes sir, actually he did this while he left for the office last week, so that is a valid reason that we can give today. We would say that he locked us inside but we won't be saying he locked us in today.

Simer: See, we are not lying.

For a moment he went quiet and then he burst into laughter, the girl at the front seat smiled and seeing her Simer laughed loudly getting excited.

Driver: *Funny guysh…*

Till the point we reached our destination Simer and I narrated all the incidents that happened whenever we got late and they were both laughing with us. Finally we reached our office, came out of his car and thanked him. We were about to move when he called us and said.

"Hey guysh! Niiiche meeting you. I am Anant khanna shenior head from recruitment team and from your company. Shee you guysh in affice. Take care." Smiling he went off in a flash.

For a moment we were both stunned with our eyes popping out

in shock, we stared at each other and then at his car that sped away.

We were 45 minutes late this time; we were seeing the class concentrating hard on the words being thrown out by the new trainer through the glass in the door. We opened the door quietly and noticed the middle aged strict trainer this time shouting and warning the class pointing out with the marker in his right hand.

"You should all be in time. I hate late comers and simple words I won't entertain any of you coming …."

"May we come in sirrrrr?" I said interrupting his warning.

He turned towards us and looking through his glasses he gave us a long stare. The whole class was now staring at us and many were trying to press their laughter and funny smile on seeing us as if we were jokers.

"Who are you? " The trainer asked in surprise as if we were aliens asking for his approval after sudden spaceship landing.

"Trainers" Simer responded quickly.

I looked at Simer abruptly wondering at his stupid reply and that too stated so confidently that for a second I thought it was true.

"Oh so you are trainers?" Then who the hell am I? He stated aggressively.

"No…no…No….sir…aaa…aa…he means we are trainees and we are from same batch." I said getting fluttered and punched Simer on the back.

"Yess...Yess sir....trainees...we are trainees..." Simer bumbled.

"Why are you late boys?" He asked getting calm. The whole class was giggling and whispering. We even saw our group pointing, teasing us, smiling and laughing putting their hand on the mouth.

"Sir aaa..We were......aa...a..a... with recruitment head and he got late." I replied forgetting the actual reason we planned to give today.

"What kind of reason is this? I didn't get you. Who recruitment head?" He asked getting fumed.

"Sir actually, we took a lift from Anant sir and he had some work on the way and because of that we got late." Simer quickly jumped in and gave a confident look after stating the reason.

He paused for moment, looked at us thinking something, removed his specs turned towards the class and said.

"Are these the same guys whom I was talking about? Every trainer has been warned of the innovative reasons they give after getting late."

The class just nodded hiding their smiles and he turned towards us and shouted.

"You two! Just move in and next time I guess you won't be late."

We apologised and moved in; we attended the lecture as alert as if we were taking some exam that very day. It was difficult though. We were not used to sitting in one place for long. Simer wanted to move out every single minute to be with Sonal. Even I missed Riya and wanted to be with her. There was something about her that had cast a magical spell on me. Whenever I managed to put her thoughts out of my mind I would get a message or call from her. She would often give missed calls in between the lectures trying to tease me, or send some funny messages. Sometimes she would ask me to come out but then she would message from class that it was just a prank.

Things were moving fast and I was feeling good to be together but sometimes thoughts of Priety would disturb me. Sometime I would feel good trying to forget and having succeeded in finding love once again. There were moments when I would console myself that things were wonderful and under control and I had moved on but the next moment I would feel like a loner searching for something that didn't exist. I wanted to change but was at that stage where I was confused and scared of the subtle changes around me. I wanted to forget her but my heart wanted to retain her forever in my life. The battle between the past and present was blocking the future from being certain and predictable.

Simer on the other side was still trying to cultivate the harmonious feelings in Sonal. Every time he would ask her to come alone for a date she would refuse, so we sought Riya's favour in persuading her for an evening out. After reaching home from office Simer would start getting ready again to meet his girl. We then used to roam around nearby their place or sit in CCD.

"Is there any airport around…?" Simer asked sonal.

"No"

'Then why is my heart ready to take off?" Simer replied flirting with her.

While sitting next to her, every alternate moment he would come up with such flirtatious comments clearly indicating to her his intentions about but she would smile, sometimes feel shy but would never thought of taking them seriously. Directly or indirectly Simer would question her about her feelings for him and one evening she finally stated.

"*hum apni dosti aage nahi badha sakte*. (We can't take our friendship further)".

Simer went quiet for a moment and then said.

"*Kyu aage meein peh riha hai…* (Is it raining ahead?)"

"Shut up! Simer. You are nice but I am still tucked in my past and I know he will be back soon and he is even from our caste….. I am …really…..sor…sorry…Please…" She said and went out trying to control her emotions.

Riya I and were absolutely shocked seeing her like this. Simer was stunned and I know he was shattered too. But he was the guy who wouldn't be lamenting and crying like an insane person. So before we could say anything to him he smiled and lifted himself up from sudden daze. He took out a chocolate from his pocket, handed it to Riya and said.

"Please give her this, and say her that it's ok and don't be upset. I want her to be my friend and I wish her good luck in future."

He stood up and was about to move and before I could say something he added.

"Please don't forget to tell her that I will never interfere in her life. I want her to be happy."

For the first time I saw Simer so serious as I could feel his pain and knew he was hurt. We moved out and Riya paced up to check if Sonal was fine. Simer shared his feelings, how he had lost his love in the past. That day he shared everything and I guess I noticed a different friend with me. He didn't cry but was broken. We reached our flat late that night. Simer called Sonal to make her feel better and felt relieved after a chat with her. We slept late and had some soft drinks with Maggie cooked by me for him. He was feeling fine and we watched as usual our favorite Punjabi dubbed Hollywood movie and Simer imitated his favourite character 'chacha Khrich' from Spiderman.

For a few days he seemed quiet and controlled but soon than he was back to business and in search of a new girl. He would try his best not on one but on many.

A girl would pull out her phone and Simer would say.

"Do you have the feature of saving my number in your cell?"

"There must be something wrong with my eyes...."

"If I were be a traffic signal, I would turn red every time you passed....." and there were many, some were mixed with filmy dialogues and others were his own inventions. They were not for one

149

but for all the girls who came in contact with him. He was a perfect entertainer and a comic flirt. Every time Riya and I were be together he would come along with a new girl introducing us to her. The next time he would come alone. But he never resented of them ditching him.

"What are you doing tomorrow?" Riya called and asked.

"Nothing!"

"Alright, let's go out for a movie then." She sounded excited.

"My favorite Ranbir kapoor is on screen again. Yipee….." She added.

Oh god! How lucky that guy is? He would take all the money from directors and producers leaving these girls dying day and night for him. But why was I thinking that way, I wondered if I was jealous. But why would I be, he wouldn't come out of the screen and take Riya with him leaving me with open wide eyes and popcorn sticking between my lips.

"Alright! No problem. I will search and let you know the timings and then we can fix a programme."

"Wow! You are smart! ….*Shining in the shade of sun like a pearl upon the ocean…hmmmmm hmmmmm hmmmmm.* Nice song na…" she asked.

"Yes…Yes very nice….." I said and then we hung up after deciding to call in the evening.

Puneet: So man! This time movieeeeee…..great man! (He said removing his earphones)

Simer revealed my plan and like always everybody was offering their valuable suggestions.

Varun: This time you must propose to her.

Me: Guys, are you crazy? Every time you say propose and all, I don't love her, we are just friens.

Puneet: Ohhhh hooooo friends! I never used to admit when I was in love with Ritu, it just feels good to hide….. But man! We are your friends and experienced toooo..

Vikas: *Oh eh pagal hai, wada experience da lagda*……. (Oh he is crazy, shouting about his experience….)

Puneet: You are insane pig…..fuck off…

Vikas: *Dafa ho saleya….teri phen*****.....fuck off…..

Varun: Shut up ….. Fools….!

Simer: Why are you reluctant to propose to her. She is a nice girl and it seems that she likes you.

Me: Ya she is nice but…..I don't love….and she just treats me like a friend…..she doesn't like…..I mean….

Puneet: I was also confused like that but be a man! You should go for her like I did and see we are engaged and getting married in a fortnight.

Vikas: Oh don't listen to him….he is fool…be a man!

Puneet gave him a stern look and was about to go to Vikas's room when he got a call from his lady love and he went out to answer the call. Simer and Varun went on to prepare dinner and left me thinking of Riya.

2007 Chandigarh:

Priety and I had a big fight this time and it took me three weeks to pacify her. Finally she was ready to go out for a movie with me only when I convinced her that she resembled Kareena Kapoor in *Jab we met*. I reached Mohali Phase 9 to pick her up but she had voiced never ever to sit on my bike. So I had to park my bike in the market and we took an auto to sector-17. To impress her I planned everything and booked the tickets for the movie in an advance.

Priety was quiet the whole way. She was not chattering as usual and worried, I was trying hard to make her talk. I would say something and she would smile, I would crack a joke and she would laugh but that bubbly Priety was missing. It was always that after a big fight I had to do something great to impress her and bring her back to normal where she would be firing me, finding faults and constantly blabbing. We reached Fun Republic well on time. The movie was about to start and she was excited now. As we were about to move I checked my pockets to find the tickets missing. I went to washroom and checked thoroughly but all in vain. I had left the tickets on the shelf before going out, I now remembered.

Oh no! Priety would now kill me. I washed my face quickly and gathering all my confidence came out and said to her.

Oh Priety! Priety!. I just checked and got it wrong. The show starts one hour later. Let's just sit.

"What the hell is this? Why didn't you tell me?" She replied, furious.

"Hey please don't get angry now. I want to spend some good time with you." Please lets sit here. I pleaded romantically.

She thought for a moment gave a suspicious look and then smiled and nodded. We occupied seats in McDonalds and I went to order the meal. After ordering I quickly went out to buy another set of tickets. I was literally praying that I would get then. I went at the ticket counter and asked for two tickets for *Jab we met* but to make things worse tickets were sold out and I was left cursing for not picking up the tickets from the shelf. I was wondering how to handle priety now. She would kill me, feared I never wanted to go inside, in fact I thought of running back and switching my cell off. How stupid of me? I was actually feeling lost when a strange voice called me from behind.

"Excuse me sir."

I turned in surprise.

"Sir I guess you need two tickets for *Jab we met*. I have five." He said smiling at me,

"Oh great! Thanks a lot. ....Yess..yesss I need two." I said feeling excited.

I was more than happy to get the tickets and excitedly I went inside. Priety was waiting anxiously and inquired why I was so late but I covered up saying that I had got an emergency call.

"You have an emergency calls only when I am with you. Now you will not attend any call. Do you understand?" She ordered.

I smiled, nodded and looked at her. I was thinking as to how messy it would have been if that person had not sold his tickets to me. How would I have been able to face her? She would have thrashed me and the crowd here would have witnessed the best drama in which a guy was being chopped for forgetting movie tickets.

"Thank God!" I whispered and looked at heaven.

"What? Why thank God? You are again ...."

"Oh no priety...thank God that you are here with me.....after our last fight I thought that I lost you....don't get angry now... I never feel my beat right when you get angry" I interrupted her placing my fingers on her hand.

She smiled and then moved her hand away looking around her and then said.

"Let's eat now my *bandar*...."

We had a great hour there when I expressed my feelings as to how I had missed her during our long fight, when I used to sit and think of her again and again, how much I cried, how crazy I had become, and how lost I had been. She was listening me, smiling at me and I noticed the glitter in her eyes. She loved to listen to me when I declared my feelings and let her know about the void in me without her. She then kicked me under the table and biting her lip she raised her eyebrow and then winked. It was her way of getting cozy in public and asking me to just be quiet. It was just like placing her finger on my lip and kissing it to make me feel that she liked that and she really cared for me. She also confessed how much she had missed me and how her anger always spoiled everything.

It was her turn to make me feel good and let me know how much she thought of me. We went for the movie then.

She was excited and from the point Kareena missed her train, her jabbering and her conversation with the stationmaster and Shahid Kapoor to the point where they take a room with Shahid negotiating with the lodge owner and Kareena saying '*2 ghante ke liye chahiye*' Priety was convinced that she actually resembled her. But before she could realize the fact I was more or less damn sure about Priety being like her she asked me abruptly.

"*Iska matlab kya hai? Ek raat ke liye kya*......why are people laughing?

"Shhhh......I will tell you later......." I whispered.

I was concentrating hard on the movie but couldn't resist stealing a glance at her now and then. Her reactions, her expressions and her emotions varied with that of Kareena's. She would smile, laugh and then hopping up and down at the song '*yeh ishq haye, jannat dikhaye*' and I trying to get her down and asking her to relax. She ordered me to bring some corn for her during the interval, preferring to stay on seat. I took the order and went to get it for my lady. I was having a great time and prayed to God to slow down the hands of the clock.

"Here is your corn? And your Fanta." I smiled handing them to her.

Priety was so stunned, that for a few minutes she was quiet and didn't say anything. She kept sitting and watching the movie without the same enthusiasm. I looked at her and asked her the reason of this.

"I ordered corns and you have brought popcorn." She lamented.

Oh no! How could I forget it? It's just that when things are going fine with me I always spoil them myself. She liked 'masala corn' and I had forgotten in excitement. And I knew she wouldn't have them and keep on sitting like that. Priety was like a kid who had not been allowed to have a balloon. If she sat like that how would I enjoy the movie? I pulled my cell out from my pocket dialled a number and slipped out of the hall. I returned after a few minutes and Priety gave an irritated look and said.

"How many times have I told you not to attend the call?"

"Here is your corn." I smiled.

That moved her, she paused for a few seconds and said,

"You stupid! I thought you went to answer a call......oh I'm sorry......."

"Shhh.... Now enjoy yourself my love and watch Kareena." I whispered and smiled.

She was back to her bubbly self again and seeing her happy I felt great. She was now holding my arm tightly now and then putting some corns into my mouth and having some herself. Finally the film ended with Shaheed-Kareena's lip lock and she pinched my arm pressing my hand tightly. Happy ending and I was expecting my future to be as happy as the conclusion of the film.

We took a bus from Fun Republic to 17 sec, she kept her head on my shoulder on the way and I was feeling her warmth and care. At 17 we took an auto to Mohali phase-9. She asked me on the way.

"How was your day lover boy?"

"Fine"

"No I mean I hope you enjoyed yourself with me." She asked.

"Of course I loved it." I assured her. Few minutes silence and then I asked the same question.

"Hey Priety! Did you enjoy yourself with me?"

She paused, stared at me and then asked me to come closer. She raised her right hand and softly placing it on my left cheek, moved her lips close to my face and kissed me on my cheek.

"I loved it when you bought corns for me."

We then held each other's hand tightly, she kept her head on my shoulder and I placed my head on her and closed my eyes, even the loud auto noise seemed like a romantic music.

Back to Pune:

So the moment came. Riya and I decided to meet at E-square for her favourite Ranbir Kapoor movie. I reached fifteen minutes before her and was wondering why I used to get late only when I was supposed to meet Priety. Before she could come I thought of buying tickets for the show. It was 12.30 and I booked for the 2 o clock show thinking that I would spend some time with Riya to create that perfect environment for the movie.

She reached and apologized a hundred times for being late, though I never wanted her to. Priety would never have said sorry despite being late; she would have given a whack at me only for any other reason. We took a seat near the food stalls above, and Riya started to tell me about her roommates and their boyfriends.

"Did you miss me?" She asked abruptly.

I was taken aback at her question but before I could answer anything she stated.

"Oh just joking.....*aiwe hi puch liya*......as in ...."she smiled.

I too smiled but nervously. Why did she ask me this question suddenly? What was wrong with her? Oh such a weird situation. I did not know what to ask or say. It seemed that I knew everything about her, and now there was nothing more left. I wanted to enjoy her conversation, but all in vain. She also noticed something unusual about me and went quiet after sometime. During the last fifteen minutes of the movie there was silence between the two of us. I excused myself pretending to answer a call and came out; hundreds of questions were running inside my mind. I should be happy that I am with someone who is not just beautiful but nice too. Riya and her talking should be in my mind and I should entertain her whole heartedly. I spent two minutes on self counselling and tried to fill my mind with admiring things about her and went back. I went and asked her smilingly.

"Would my princess like to have anything else?"

"What? Princess ....as in......?" she inquired tying her loose hair with the band in between her teeth and looking through her glasses at me.

"Just leave them loose, they look good that way." I said.

"What's wrong with you?" She asked in surprise, smiling and threw a folded paper napkin at me.

"Nothing. Alright let's have your favorite strawberry ice cream before we go in." I said excitedly and went to buy one for her. She didn't tie her hair after that, I must admit she was looking stunning with the silky smooth hair like a halo round her face and her ravishing light pink top fitting her slender figure perfectly.

The movie began and the crowd expected a lot from Ranbir and Katrina, I too had great expectations, not from the stars on 70mm but from Riya. I was trying hard but not to watch the movie but

Riya, moving my eyes from the big screen to the beauty sitting next to me. She was watching the movie quietly, with no enthusiasm except she would smile whenever Ranbir would hit the screen with his charm. She would laugh at his joke and crossing her legs she would keep her elbow on her right thigh chin supported with her hand upright and staring at Ranbir like a mad lover. I wanted her to laugh whole heartedly, make comparisons, disturb me, ask me, pop up and down on her seat. She should react at every scene, ask me some dumb questions and try to predict the movie but she was mum. I kept rolling my eyes at the movie, then at Riya then at the movie then again at the Riya. But I guess I was a fool expecting the same. The interval came and we moved out. I went quickly and bought 'masala corn' for her but to my surprise she didn't like the corn. Instead she insisted on popcorn with chocolate flavour.

The movie ended on a positive note.

"Nice movie na!" She asked pinching me.

"Ya but I guess it was impractical." I stated getting aggressive.

"What? Don't you dare state anything about my Ranbir's movie? It was awesome. I love himmm." She stated.

"Yes it was impractical, totally impractical. How an uneducated, worthless and unemployed guy get a girl? No status and no match. There should be some practicality and it would have been right if the girl had left him and married that rich guy......I hope you understood."

She was stunned for few minutes, stared at me with eyes popping out and then laughed suddenly.

"Wow! What a lecture? Wah! Wah! Mr. Practical. It was just a movie. *Senti ho gayeee*......" she laughed.

I got so aggressive which I never expected. Why was I taking the film so critically? After all it was a movie just for our entertainment. The film was nice but I never wanted to accept it and that too just because I was needlessly relating myself with the situation in it. Like any other odd guy I was trying to relate myself to the character of the movie.

We roamed around for an hour there and she was as usual chatting and trying to lighten my mood which I had spoiled without any reason. I also tried then to crack a few jokes and make her feel good. We then took an auto upto Vishal Nagar. We were sitting quietly and then she asked.

"Hey! You enjoyed yourself with me na! I think you got bored. Haina....tell ....pls"

I quickly went back in a flash thinking of the whole day and felt guilty for making her feel like that. Just for a second I was reminded of the same question asked by Priety after '*jab we met*'and I remember how she responded when I asked the same. So I smiled gazing at her, asked her to come close to me and then placing my left hand on her right cheek I moved my lips near her soft glowing cheek just to feel the wondrous silky touch and thanked her for being with me. She smiled and then turned her look outside.

"Riya!" I called her name like never before getting close to her ear whispering softly with all the intense feelings I could.

"I hope I didn't bore you." I asked softly and in a lower voice feeling guilty.

Biting her lower lip she turned towards me, and adjusting her hair blown by the wind with her right hand she gave a magnetic smile and then asked me to close my eyes. I did and felt her smooth right hand touching my left cheek and her ever glossy soft lips with light breath just touching and feeling my right cheek and whispering she stated.

"Thanks for being with me too."

I reached home and everybody started to inquire about the date. I was quiet and tired, I only told them about the movie and went to bed. I was about to sleep when my cell beeped and it was a message from Riya.

"*Hey! Missing you.*

Sweet dreams."

I wanted to answer her but again the battle between past and present started and I don't know why I got confused and felt guilty. I tried to ignore the message and closed my eyes thinking of the whole day spent with Riya. But Priety's thoughts were forcefully taking all the space and kicking out what could be my present and future.

FORBIDDEN KISS

Simer was excited to leave for Mumbai after office as Sonal had invited him on her birthday. So he was packing his bags the night before and discussing about her gift. We slept late that night and as a result we woke up late next morning and again late for the class. We were on our way when we received a message from our Punjab group about the mock test which was scheduled the same day by our new trainer who was taking the classes of J2EE. We were really shocked to find that we had both forgotten about it. We were blaming each other for not remembering about the exam. We knew we would be screwed up as we were late by half an hour and that too for the test which was supposed to be taken seriously.

"Hell man! Keep on crying about Mumbai, see now we are late."

I said angrily.

"*Main ki kita pai, what's wrong with you man?*" Simer defended himself.

"Sonal, Mumbai, date and all….. Vikas is right, you hardly think about your career and company. Just see now we have missed our test." I blamed Simer.

"Oh look who is talking……? Who keeps on searching love here and there all the time?" Simer retorted.

"Shut up!"

"Now, what to do?" Simer asked.

"Wait! Hold on. We need to make a plan." I said.

"I hate your fucking plans…… they are always weird and pointless." Simer fired.

I gave a cross look turning towards him as we were walking briskly towards the lecture room.

"But I guess we don't have any other option." I said.

"Now listen. You won't say a single word; just behave as if you are ill for the last few days. Change your expression." I added.

"Expression! You mean I should look sick." Simer inquired.

Simer at once changed his expression to a pale, off colour person with eyes showing his weakness. He kept his mouth open to show how out of breath he was after such an illness. By God, he was a damn good actor.

"May we come in sirrrrr?" I asked gently after pushing the door open.

"Hey....*itna late kayise*! Where were you?" The trainer asked in surprise.

"Sir actually, my friend is not well. He had something last night which resulted in food poisoning and the whole night he struggled and finally we went to the doctor in the morning. So that's why we got late." I said confidently.

Simer initially kept his hand on his forehead but as soon as I said food poisoning, he abruptly kept his hand on his stomach. He was so natural that for a moment I wondered whether he really had an attack of food poisoning.

The trainer was yet to be convinced as he doubted our excuse so he asked me to get the permission from the HR head.

"Ok sir, where is his office?" I asked.

Though we knew but still we took his address expecting that he may gave us a chance and started to move to get the permission and Simer whispered.

"*Lao daso*....see you're fucking plan ...I told you....shit.... "

I was about to pull the door and move out when the trainer called again.

"Just listen."

"Yes sir." I said turning towards him pretending to be clean-handed.

"Are you prepared for the test?"

I paused, looked at simer and replied confidently.

"Yes sir. Both of us have prepared."

"Alright, just go and sit at the back and revise. Let the whole class finish their test. Sit quietly." He advised.

We immediately followed his instruction and ran to occupy the last seats of the room. We were excited but controlled our emotions for our rubbish plan actually worked in our favor. For the next half an hour Simer kept his head down and was pretending to be sick. The trainer came to us and asked Simer.

"What did you have last night?"

"Sir...wo ....a...aa." simer raised his head and fluttered.

"Sir vada pao." I responded interrupting Simer.

"Yes sir vada pao from a street vendor, I guess that's why I got sick." Simer added quickly.

"The street vendors don't have quality food. Next time just be careful." The trainer advised and went back to his seat.

We heaved a sigh of relief, Simer was giggling but somehow he curbed himself and kept on pretending to be sick. A few minutes passed and the trainer again came and asked Simer.

"What did you have for dinner last night?"

"Sir a.. aa...a.." Simer bumbled again.

"Sir daal makhani" I quickly responded.

"Yes sir daal makhani from dhaba, that's why I got sick." simer added and then kept his head down.

"You should not have anything from dhaba, they don't have quality food. Be careful next time". He advised again and went back.

Simer stared at me and I knew I had made a mistake by changing the dish. We were happy and enjoying the success of our plan and escaping the test. Simer got busy chatting with Sonal and sending flirting messages alongside to other girls and I also got busy with Riya on text messages. We didn't notice how and when the trainer came and interrupted us. Seeing him Simer changed his expressions at once and I turned towards him to pay some extra attention to my dear sick friend. The trainer again asked the same question but this time in a different way and we both were completely stumped as we were bit extra conscious of the doubt that he might have seen us chatting on cell.

"Sir we had a..a……" simer faltered again.

"Sir we had kadi pakora for dinner." I cut simer abruptly.

We both paused after my last line wondering that he might get suspicious. We both stared at him expecting something harsh.

"Oh kadi pakora is always bad for stomach. You should not eat that." The trainer advised again.

"Yes sir kadi pakora from dhaba, that's why I got sick" Simer added and then kept his head down like never to raise it again and left me to face the trainer.

The trainer smiled, nodded and before he could ask me anything one of our batch mates called him to resolve his doubt. He left and we took a sigh of relief. I guess he knew it by then after all he was the trainer and experienced too. His smile said all but it was not college where we would have been thrashed so we survived. We had an argument as simer complained of changing the dish which had made him sick every time and I defended myself arguing till the point he got a call and went out.

Simer left in the evening for Mumbai and I came back to the flat. Puneet was already there before and as usual talking to his girlfriend on the mobile. I guess they were busy planning their wedding. I heard Puneet talking about her bridal dress, the color of his sherwani the farm they would be booking in Ludhiana and so on. How cute it is to discuss about it when everything is finalized and you have all the required permissions in this world to get excited about and that too infinitely?

"So how's you dude?" Puneet finally removing his earphone greeted me after half an hour of discussion with his love.

"Great man! I hope everything is finalized now about your wedding." I said smiling and moved towards the corner of the room where our cricket kit was kept.

"*Aur dulhe sahib!* How are you feeling being no more single after a week?" I added picking up the bat and pushing the tennis ball with my foot towards Puneet.

"*bahut khush hu veer, really very happy, excited and nervous too.*" Puneet replied smiling picking up the ball with his right hand.

Puneet and I used to play cricket everyday in our room. We would go for series of five to ten matches ending up exhausting ourselves. That was our '*kamra*' cricket named by Simer which had all the exceptional rules to keep us interested enough to engage ourselves for hours in playing that.

"Yar being with Ritu is like a dream come true. I really feel sometime fortunate to get my love." Puneet said excitedly and bowled to me.

"Hey nice! *Waise* how and when did you meet her?" I asked after playing the shot for four.

"We were colleagues in office and good friends." He replied and paused and then said again teasing me.

"Like you and Riya are."

I gave him an unusual smile, stared at him shaking my head and ignoring his comment I sighed and then asked him to continue with his story.

"I was also confused initially and then I took the decision to propose to her as somewhere down in the bottom of my heart I knew that she was the one for me." He said.

"So, what did you do?" I asked raising eyebrows.

"Finally I took her to Hollywood Gurudwara and in Wahe Guru's supreme presence I expressed my feelings for her." He said excitedly thinking about the past, his achievement and then bowled me out.

"*Out! Yes! Yes...dekha* the power of love is with me...." He added laughing and moved towards me to take the bat.

"Yes man! The power of love is with you." I said smilingly handing him the bat and bent down to pick up the ball.

I was really happy the way he proposed and about the two of them getting married. But at the same time I wanted to be with Priety forever. I wanted to propose to her asking her about the power of her love over me. But she was no more part of my life and yet I was feeling and missing her. That seemed bit unbelievable to me. I was just bowling to him and finally lost in my thoughts I didn't see the power shot hit by him which hit me on the forehead with a loud thump. Keeping my hand on my forehead I collapsed with Puneet throwing his bat and running towards me to pick me up.

"Where were you lost man? Are you ok?" Puneet asked.

"Nothing...it's just... I am fine..." I sighed and smiled.

"Chal leave it....let me take you to Hollywood Gurudwara." Puneet said.

"Hollywood Gurudwara?" I asked rubbing my forehead.

Ya man! Get ready. Fast! He said and went to change.

We got ready, came down and he kicked his Splendor and we paced towards the sacred place. Puneet was excited and wanted to tell me about all the places where he dated his love but before he could start he received a call from Ritu as he had forgotten to call her and tell her about the floral arrangement he planned at his wedding. This resulted in is facing the wrath of his loving girlfriend oops! fiance. He tried to handle her giving valid reasons and driving the bike with one hand till he surrendered completely and asked me to drive the bike and let him convince his love sitting pillion. I could very well imagine his situation as he was handling it perfectly stating some valid lies that trying to confuse her and finally he was successful before he faced another round of her anger when he said that he was going to Hollywood Gurudwara with me.

"But sweetu, I am just going there with my friend.....I ...I remember we planned to go together....I am just.....please..." he was faltering.

I was driving and wondering how girls could be so possessive about their plans being upset by their loving boyfriends. Priety used to get pissed off with me when I used to do like this and I used to wonder how can you convince her in such a situation or explain her that why her plan got dismantled. Ritu was firing away at him and Puneet kept on requesting her to be normal and finally he shut her with an emotional tantrum, saying he was not going anywhere. That pacified her in return making Puneet win the argument and the license to enjoy himself without her. He kept his cell back in pocket, gave a sigh of relief and then said.

"Thank God! She is happy now."

I didn't ask anything as I could very well assess the situation and his feelings too. We reached Hollywood Gurudwara as Puneet guided me through the ways to the place. On reaching there Puneet started to describe the Gurudwara, where he had taken Ritu, where they had sat together and prayed. I could very well see the excitement on his face and his words meant a lot saying how much he was missing her. After all they had both promised each other to be together so still an emotional glitch was teasing him from inside of breaking the promise. We sat there inside and Puneet met one of his friends and went out.

I preferred to sit there for a while concentrating on the holy messages painted on the slides there. I don't know when my mind moved to the thoughts of Priety, my visit with her to the sacred places in Chandigarh, our evergreen thoughtful plans and Riya, then Puneet's proposing to his girlfriend. Everything was running fast in my mind. I was distracted from my thoughts when I read the lines.

> *Kal Kaal di chinta kar ke, tu apna aap gawaya,*
> *Aj da simran kar le, bhagta satguru nanak paya*

You have lost yourself thinking of tomorrow and past,

Just live the present and attain the Almighty'.

The slide moved but I was stick with those lines conveying the deep meaning. I was thinking hard, Was that a message from God? I should be out of the past now. I should concentrate on the present. I was applying the same thought on the current life I was dealing with. I should admire what I have in my present and that is Riya or I should give time to myself. Before I could figure out further Puneet came and asked me to leave for our flat.

We moved out and I was still thinking about Riya. Puneet was driving this time as there were no more calls from his girlfriend. So he was excitedly showing me places where he had dated her. He showed me MacD in Deccan where he had taken her on his birthday. LBS road where they used to hang out often, Dilasa restaurant where they dine together, Data Road, Mhatre Bridge and SB Road hostel. He described each and every incident related to the places where he had gone for a date with her and he was really missing those moments. For a moment I forgot everything and was enjoying his description imagining myself with my girl. My dream could hardly last for few moments when I was distracted by message in my cell. It was from Riya.

"Call me whenever you get free. Urgent!"

We reached the flat, Puneet went on to park the bike and I dialled her number as per her message.

"Hey! How are you?" She said excitedly.

"Hey Riya! You messaged. I hope things are fine." I asked.

"Ha re buddhu! *Aise hi kiya tha...*" she said smilingly.

"Are you free tomorrow?" She asked.

"Yes I am. But why?" I asked.

"Alright, then you are coming here to my flat and will teach me salsa." She said in a commanding voice.

"What? Salsa? But I don't know."

"You liar, don't escape. You only told me last time that you know salsa. Now you will teach me." She said raising her voice.

"Yes but..."

"No if no but only salsa." she interrupted and laughed.

"Reach my place at 11am sharp. Ok now talk to you later." She said and hung up.

I didn't tell this to my roommates to avoid any stupid suggestions they would start to deliver after knowing about my meeting with Riya.

2007:

I went to bed quietly and was thinking about the first time when Priety came to my place during my college days. How excited I had been when she decided that she would be coming. She was coming with her mother near my residence when she pondered over the chance of meeting me.

"My mother is visiting her friend which is just a few kilometers from yours. I will try to come to your place today." Priety said excitedly.

"How will you manage Priety?" I asked.

"Simple, I would ask her that I need to get the notes from my friend's house which is nearby and will come to your place." She said.

"Wow! Great ha!" I exclaimed.

"Great na! I am clever." She said.

"Then we will lunch together." I said.

"No no, I will just come for 5-10 minutes."

"But 5-10 *minutes*, I won't be able to do anything sweetheart." I said mischievously.

"Shut up! What are you up to? I will kill you if you ever talk like that." She shouted.

I eagerly waited for the clock to strike one so that she could be at my place. Fortunately no one was there at my place so I was more excited. I messaged her the address and explained her the way to my place. Before leaving her mother she happily messaged me and said that her mother would take some time so we would be having one hour together. I changed four to five shirts and finally wore the one gifted by her to look better. Constantly looking into the mirror and combing my hair finally the clock showed the exact time that we had set. I was eagerly waiting for her call so that I could open the door. I couldn't call as per her instructions of not to call or message till she asked me to do so. Minutes passed quickly and in a flash fifteen minutes were gone. I was really getting furious, if I had been a minute late she would have killed me and just see how late she was. I wanted to shout at her and finally I gathered the confidence and dialled her number to inquire where she was. The bell rang and I was planning the dialogue to make her realize that she was late and I didn't like late comers. She picked up the call.

"Why are you….." I could say only that much.

"Where is your residence? You gave me the wrong address you fiend." She interrupted and shouted at me.

"Wrong address? Where are you Priety?" I asked politely.

I was suppose to shout at her but the plan failed and instead I pacified her and told her the exact location explaining her the way to my place, I was guiding her and she kept on instructing her driver and finally the meeting which could have lasted sixty minutes reduced to just 15 minutes. That too for five minutes Priety expressed her anger despite the fact that it was not my fault. So I had to make valiant efforts in churning up her mood and bringing her back to her normal mode. I talked, I sang, I cracked jokes and finally she laughed when I did a funny dance on Shakira's song.

She started to narrate the whole story, how she convinced her mother who was getting suspicious of my residence and how cleverly she managed to take her permission. On the other side I was sitting in front of her listening to her smiling and then shifting my position near her and more close to her. I wanted to kiss her lips which were constantly fluttering but she understood my intentions and pushed me hard.

"You fiend! I told you." She shouted.

"And you are not listening to me na. Ok bye I am going." She got up and was about to run.

"No no no Priety, I am listening." I said holding her hand and stopping her.

"Then tell what I said?" she asked moving back slightly.

Oh God again a test. She always behaved like that. Somebody should tell her that we were left with just a few minutes and she wanted me to narrate the whole incident. I held her hand more tightly and asked her to sit before I started to talk. She sat and I started.

"You were saying that your lover boy was missing you badly." I said.

"Shut up!"

"Shhhh. Let me finish." I said keeping my finger on her lips.

"Your lover boy was missing you, thinking of you, wanted to spend a few good moments with you and thinking of making a few seconds more precious with you."

We both gazed at each other and finally I took her favourite chocolate Crackle out from my pocket and said.

"A small token of sweet for my lovely angel."

She said thanks and surrendered herself to my arms and we were lost in each other. I was really feeling divine with her when her cell rang and brought us back from heavenly world.

"Oh no mummy calling. I gotta go...bye bye...."she said holding her cell and afraid as if her mother would walk out of it.

"Hello mamma, I am just coming...I...I have left. Ok."

She disconnected the call, grabbed her purse and quickly moved out after adjusting her hair.

"Don't come after me. My driver will get suspicious. Love you lover boy." She instructed and then smiled and went away.

Lover boy was just left wondering the punctuality of her mother and the interruption as if she sensed her daughter being loved at a nearby place.

Back in Pune:

I got ready and just when I was about to leave for Riya's flat at Vishal Nagar, I got her call inquiring about the same.

"Ya dear! I am just about to leave."

"Alright, then see you. byeee." She said and hung up.

I left for her place and thought of buying something for her like I always did, so I bought chocolates and her favorite strawberry ice cream. I never wanted to but still Puneet's proposal to his girlfriend and his story were all in my mind and I was thinking the same way about Riya. I just checked myself, adjusted my hair, wiped off the wrinkle on my shirt and before I could ring her door bell she opened the door.

"How the hell did you know that I am standing outside?" I asked in surprise.

"I saw through the balcony and this is for me na." she responded and snatched the packet from me in excitement as if she already knew about it.

She was looking stunning in her yellow shorts and black silky top with her loose wet hair. I had never ever seen her like that and I couldn't stop staring at her forgetting everything as if I had lost my senses. How beautiful girls can be in casual wear! And why was there any need for them to be in flashy dresses when they could kill a guy with their simple wear. I entered and looked at the very well furnished and clean rooms unlike ours rooms untidy and withered walls with plaster on walls that too showing various figures changing every day. I could hear the light music turned on in her laptop which was kept on the study table near her bed. I went near the table, pulled out the chair and sat there. I saw Riya coming from kitchen bringing a cold drink for me.

"Hello Mr. Salsa! Shall I show you my pics?" she asked.

"Get up! First grab your cold drink." She added handing me the tray in an excitement.

She took her glasses from the box in the drawer, tied her loosened hair adjusted her chair, held the mouse in her right hand and started to explore the folders in her laptop. For the next half an hour I kept on sipping the cold drink and she kept on explaining each of her pic. There was a point when I was just nodding and smiling even before she described the pic. Priety used to show me her pics with great enthusiasm and explaining even the situation. I was almost lost in priety's thoughts when Riya suddenly asked.

"You are getting bored na?" she asked softly.

"No not at all. Nice pics. I mean you look gorgeous Priety...oh sorry Riya"

She paused herself for a moment, ceased to smile and stared at me for a second and then closed the folders. Without saying a single word she got up, picked the tray and went to the kitchen. I was stunned at her behaviour but I didn't react and instead tried to ignore and kept myself busy by picking up the magazine kept on the table. After a few minutes she came back. She pulled the chair again and this time the pulling was more violent than normal. I noticed pretending to be ignorant of her sudden behaviour like that.

"I have to leave in a short while, so you can teach me salsa if you have finished your reading." She said sharply exploring something on her laptop and without gazing at me.

I immediately kept the magazine aside and asked her to select the song and tried suggesting a few. Finally after shuffling through the playlists we selected one song. I could very well notice that she was not the Riya who had excitedly opened the door and greeted me. Seeing her fuming like this I could not resist asking her the reason.

"Nothing, I am just fine. You don't have to worry about me." She responded.

I remember how I made up Priety's mood so I tried the same here. I tried to divert her attention by dancing awkwardly selecting the weirdest of songs I could. She kept staring at me coldly. After failing in all the attempts I gave up and sat down on the floor folding my legs, closing my eyes, joined my hands and I started singing.

"Aarti shri Riya ji ki main gaun, tumko ardaas kare gun gaun….."

I could sing only that much in my pathetic voice when she burst into laughter and stood up to clap and was on track.

"Will you teach me salsa or shall I beat you?" She smiled and punched me.

I did a few steps alone first and asked her to observe so that we could collaborate and do them together. By the time I was guiding her I noticed her loosening her hair removing her band and then rolling them roughly without clip or band into a bun. She seemed to be a quick learner and picked up the steps very well. After completing the warm up sessions I stretched my hand towards her. She removed her glasses, gently kept her left hand on mine and moved closer to me. I felt her slender fingers close convulsively round mine. The music was on and the rhythm was perfect as we started to move on that tune.

"ek din teri rahon mein , bajon mein, panaho mein aaunga....."

The steps matched perfectly hands in hands, movement well in coordination. The next step where I held her left hand upright and she rotated like a doll with her right hand placed at the back. Suddenly her bun came off and the loosened waves of her hair poured like a cascade from her head across my eyes, half blinding me. The fragrance completely broke my resistance. I then shuffled to the next step where I held her right hand in my left with her pressing it tightly and kept my right hand gently on her waist and we both moved bit closer to each other. Her eyes were sharply blazing at mine.

"Yeh jhukti nazar jane jigar hosh le jaati hai......"

I could hear this line of the song before I was lost completely in her and could feel her letting me feel so. She was completely set on her feet and we stood together there with both my arms round her the waist and our lips locked in the beauty of the moment. We surrendered completely to each other and the moment got passionate before she hugged me tightly and whispered.

"I love you".

Oh those three words just hit me hard and I was conscious now. With the sudden shock I opened my eyes and saw her holding me tightly and expecting me to say something soothing for her ears. For her it was a revelation, a complete surrender of heart and soul… her victory. But for me it was a defeat, a bitter regret. For even while my senses reeled I knew there must be a reckoning and that there was still…Priety…

I pulled out and turned away from her.

"What is it?" she murmured.

"I …am sorry…this sort of thing cannot happen between us…I should be sensible." I turned and moved towards the door.

"Is she Priety na? That's her name na?" she asked softly.

"Yes". I admitted.

"You still love her?" She asked.

"I don't know but I can't be in love with anyone. I am …just sorry…Please…" I left after saying this.

THE LAST DAY

It was the last week before our final exam to survive in the company and probably the last three days of Puneet in our flat before he could go back to Punjab to tie the knot with his girlfriend. Simer was back from Mumbai and he seemed bit serious about the exam this time. But I was lost somewhere; the mind was behaving like a pendulum swinging to and fro between Riya and Priety. The conflict between past and present was killing me. I was getting irritated at small things, was hardly concentrating on the lectures and preferred to be alone most of the time. Three days passed and I didn't see Riya at all, neither called her and she did the same. Half of me wanted me to call her and ask about her while the other half was contented without her.

It was the last day of Puneet at the flat. He already got his luggage and things shifted to his new flat before leaving for his native place. All of us came down to see him off after cutting the farewell cake in our flat. It had been nice having Puneet with and we knew we would be missing him. He hugged us all turn by turn wise and when he came towards me he said.

"Why do you seem lost man?" He asked while hugging me.

"Its because you are going, that's why." I said smiling gently but not looking into his eyes.

"No dude! I think you are in love." he teased me and added while sitting inside the auto.

"Seriously man! Go and propose to Riya." He said and then winked at me smiling as if he knew what was going on.

"And guys I want you all to be present at my marriage. See you there in Punjab. Bye take care." he shouted while the auto he boarded took off.

"Are you fine? Even we are noticing something unusual about you." Varun asked after Puneet left.

"I am fine yar. It's just that the exam is on and I need to study hard to survive." I said covering up the real tremor I was facing.

I tried to prepare hard for the exam this time and finally the exam day came and the result as expected was not in my favour. I flunked again. I was under more pressure as things did not seem in my favour. I left for the flat early without letting Simer know about it. The disturbed personal life was affecting my career line badly. Nothing was in my mind at that point of time except the thought of failing in my exam. I thought myself being thrown out of the company when I received a call from Simer. I was not in a mood to talk so I preferred not to answer it. He kept on calling and I kept on ignoring the calls. I wanted to rest in peace and but before I could give rest to my mind the door bell rang. I ran to open the door only to find Varun with a strange expression.

"Oh man! You are here. Simer was madly looking for you in the company. Why are you not picking up his calls?" Varun said angrily entering the room.

"Ya I came here.....a.. and..and I was sleeping." I faltered.

"There is something wrong with you. You have to tell me, I can't be wrong as I have been watching you since last week." Varun asked after keeping his bag down on the floor of his room.

I couldn't control my expressions as they clearly showed the pain on my face. So I broke down and narrated everything and the situation I was facing. Varun heard me patiently and then consoled me.

"It was you only who wanted to fall in love again. So why are you running away from it now?" Varun expressed.

"I can understand what you went through, I too faced a similar situation when my love left me only to get married somewhere else but it was then that I decided to move on and never ever to love again." he added before he paused and then started again.

"Neither had I tried nor did I get any opportunity to find love in my life but dude you are fortunate enough to get another chance. Riya seemed to be a nice girl. She loves you and now you should not lose her"

"Yes dude! You should go for her." Simer also jumped in as he was hearing everything and couldn't resist from giving me free advice.

I kept on thinking about Riya and my feelings towards her. I was self analyzing everything, trying to support the fact about her and trying to make up my mind about love again. It's the time now that I should give up my past and create some more space for the present. Things were getting clear and I was getting relieved but then the failure in my exam and fear of exit from the company picked up and I was anxious again.

"But I have failed in my exam and I guess according to the policy I will be out of the company and how would Riya…." I let out my fear.

"Congrats man! You are safe." Simer interrupted me.

Simer calculated the average of the last and the previous exam and that was the reason that he was calling me. As per the criteria the average of both the exams should be above the deadline and fortunately I was just on the edge but I was safe. That congratulation made me more positive and I felt the ray of bright light even on my personal life too.

"Thanks guys! You are my great friends. Thanks a lot." I just hugged them and then Varun shouted.

"Oye bring the cake guys"

The next day I was eagerly waiting to meet Riya and admit my feelings towards her. It was the whole last week that I couldn't see her so the excitement to meet her and confessing was more and I was getting impatient too. I didn't call her to give her surprise so I better preferred to wait a bit more so as to encounter the beautiful smile on her face. The whole batch seemed happy too as the exams were over, the training period passed off and after clearing the exam we all were now employees of the esteemed organization. So before the projects being allotted to everyone in different locations around India, the fresh employees were busy in clicking the pics and capturing the happiest training moments in their cams. Everybody was enjoying and an element of separation after the allocation was in their mind too but still the celebrations were on. There were consolations and motivations for the few who missed to pass the exam. I also enjoyed with group but was now missing Riya. I couldn't resist myself before I called her only to get the message of her phone switched off, so I called sonal out from her bay to get information about Riya.

"Riya is in Mumbai" Sonal replied.

"Why? What happened?"

"She went to Mumbai last week and was on leave for the whole of last week. I guess she would be coming by the evening today." she replied before she went on to continue with her work.

I was left in a state of ambiguous questions about Riya's absence and her leave the whole of last week. I was wondering about the reason, my mind was full of a thousand fears, doubts and confusions. I sat in the lawn near the front gate so as to catch her as soon as she arrived. I was a bit worried and wondering as to how she would react, seeing me after that incident. After waiting for two long hours I saw her entering with her bag and purse. I guess she had come to the office directly from the airport. I ran towards her quickly and shouted her name. She turned back, smiled and responded calmly.

"Hey, how are you?" she asked.

"I am fine. How are you?" I asked after replying.

"I am fine too." She responded softly and smiling. I didn't notice any glum expressions or any sign that she was avoiding me.

"Where have you been last week? Why did you take leave suddenly?" I asked immediately.

At once she frowned when I asked that question and she stared coldly at me and said she would talk to me after half an hour. She went away and I was left with no choice to wait for another half an hour to know reason about her sudden absence. I was actually cursing myself as held myself responsible for her leave. That half an hour was absolutely unbearable. Finally the cell rang and it was Riya. She asked me to come near the back of the building-2 where we often used to sit sipping tea.

I reached there and could see her sitting and as usual looking fine in her glasses and adjusting her hair.

"I am sorry." I said without making eye contact with her.

"I wanted to say you something as I…."

I could say only that much when she interrupted and said boldly.

"I have resigned from the company and today is my last day"

I was absolutely stunned and could only gape at her. Finally I asked.

"What? Why?"

"My parents finally got separated and my mother is the worst affected of the two. So we have decided to move to USA to my maternal uncle."

She seemed to be in deep pain while saying this. She was looking here and there, not making eye contact with me and I could see her voice getting choked and her eyes brimmed over with tears.

"How can my father slap my mother? Disgusting!" She broke down and started crying.

I wanted to hug her and tell her that I was with her and loved her but couldn't. I tried to console her but was completely running out of words to pacify her, to cheer her. Even I felt like broken and down.

She would be going as she had resigned and this was our last meeting. This was unexpected as I came here to make my and her life different but destiny has something else. It was already 6 o clock by then and she wiped her tears, picked her bag and took something out from it.

"A gift for you. You have been special to me. I will always remember you." She said, handing me the small packet and started to move away.

I was left speechless seeing her crying like this and a token of love from her side. I gathered confidence and stopped her.

"Please don't go. I will miss you and I…. I love you Riya."

She stopped at once, turned, stared at me for a few seconds, smiled and moved a few inches closer to me.

"I confessed my feeling for you and I still mean it but at this point of time I can't be selfish. My mother needs me more than anybody else." She said softly looking into my eyes.

I could sense the love and feeling of resentment too in her eyes. I was a mere listener. I could not think of anything I could say to stop her. I want to cry at that point of time but controlled myself.

"You still love Priety. And shall I say one thing?" She added with confidence.

I looked at her in despair and nodded.

"You must give yourself some time and try to move on. You seemed stick in your past and that is holding you back. Just move on and be happy."

"And I will really miss you. Take care."

These were the last words from her and I saw her slowly getting out of my sight forever leaving me standing with a feeling of emptiness within.

It seemed that history was repeating itself. My last meeting with Priety had left me in same situation when I was about to leave for Pune from jalandhar two months ago for an MNC.

2009:

I remember Priety had called the same day had I resigned from the previous company. She knew that I was leaving the next morning. She wanted to meet me for the last time as we both knew that we wouldn't be able to meet in future. I didn't want to see her, but couldn't refuse her. So we decided to see each other for the last time at the bus stand. We chose this so as to avoid any hiccups as she couldn't meet me in any of the restaurants or CCDs.

As usual I was late but this time she was not angry rather she was a bit quiet and smiling.

"The traffic was too much and I needed to pack my luggage also."

"Did I ask for any clarification?" Raising her eyebrows she said in a calm way.

"Hey Priety! A last gift from your lover boy."

Her attention was grabbed and I was saved but she was looking into my eyes and I could feel her beauty. The mesmerizing eyes which were so genuine, so honest, so deep and far too beautiful to be resisted.

Before taking my gift she handed me something and asked me to open it there only. So we opened our gifts together and we both were surprised to see each other's gift. She had gifted me a copy of *Bhagwad Geeta* and I had gifted her an idol of lord Krishna. No doubt I was furious with GOD at that stage but still had some trust in him not for my sake but for her's so the lord who scripted and witnessed each and every moment of our story was being exchanged in different way. One got the words in the form of a book and the other got the narrator as an image.

"Best of luck and always be the same as you are now!" I said.

Before she could reply I asked innocently.

"Will you ever miss me?"

She nodded before I could bid her a final goodbye; I noticed tears trickling down her cheek. I didn't want her to cry as I couldn't see her crying and she knew this. I was trying very hard to be strong and not let my emotions out. Would somebody tell her how cute she was looking, I wanted to hug her, I wanted to wipe her tears away as I had done but the fact was I had lost all the rights now. She was fumbling while crying as she always did, like a kid.

Oh god all her words seemed to be haunting me at that time, in a flash I saw all the quality time spent with her. Our talks, our fights, our love, our first kiss, her anger, her questions, my answers and at last this moment here where we were waving each other for ever. Oh god! I was feeling like a destitute.

'I will miss you'

These were the last words from her when I was brought back to my senses. I wanted her to leave then as it was really getting tougher for me to hold back my tears. But I put up a brave front and a fake smile. I wanted to tell her many things but I couldn't. I prepared many farewell quotes but none came out. In fact I was stumped by the situation I was facing. The excitement was gone, the confidence was shattered, the eyes were getting numb and the throat was choked.

I don't know what prompted her but she asked me to sing the song that she loved to hear from me. I couldn't I wanted to say but I wanted to sing for her for the last time. I started

'main koi aisa geet gaun ke arzoo jagaun ,

agar tum kaho, ke tumko bulau ,

ke palke bichau , kadam tum jahan jahan……….'

I couldn't complete the last line as my throat was completely filled. If I had been alone I would have cried like never before. She cried even more and then I took a last sight of her and waved her good bye. I still remember the touch. I walked as briskly as I could. For her I was gone in a flash but I was hiding there just to see her boarding the car.

"Please don't go Priety. Please don't go. I love you. Give me some time and I will be something soon. Please wait......." These were the words that I wanted her to hear.

The car engine ignited and Priety was gone. The most beautiful chapter of my life was closed with a never ending conclusion. The love story I wanted to script perfectly with a happy ending was left incomplete with destiny penning the emptiness in my life and finally tears were out after a long wait and I cried.

Back in pune:

The next day I got a mail of my transfer to the new location and that was Greater Noida. Finally I was allotted a project and I had to move on. So I booked the tickets for the next day. I gave this news to my roommates and they were feeling bad too. The last day came and I took a bus from Pune to Bandra to board my train from the railway station directly to New Delhi. Together with my roommates Priya, Palak, Shradha, Sonal and my Punjab group came to bid me good bye. I was smiling inside seeing the trio of engaged, committed and married. But that smile was more or less to cover up the feeling of missing them all and mostly Riya who left me two days ago.

Simer and Varun seemed very upset. First Puneet, then my transfer and I could see the pain of missing both of us was troubling them and all those precious moments together. Our suggestions, our flat, our fights and our cakes and I will be missing all.

"I will remember all your formulas to woo a girl." Simer giggled and hugged me tightly; Varun also hugged me but didn't utter a single word as eyes expressed everything he wanted to convey.

"Fuck off man! He is crazy. You take care buddy. Nice time with you." Vikas said and hugged me and they all waved me a final good bye.

I was analyzing my journey to Pune and my last few months. If I count on positives I found good friends, I survived in a company, I had a great time and most of all I met Riya. What an irony! How twist and turns combined with beauty sometimes brings your life to a point where you are left with memories of the glorious pasts and nothing else. When I started from Jalandhar I wanted to fall in love once again but on the other side I was not ready to shed the past I faced.

I made things worse when i drew comparisons between the two and wanted the Riya and others to be like Priety. Actually I was not searching for love but searching Priety in every girl I met. I wanted them to lead me, to dominate me, to always keep me running here and there, to find faults in me, to contradict their statements as Priety used to do, shout at me, get angry at me, dress like her, talk like her and so on.

Last but not the least I failed to realize and unable to accept the fact that I was still in love with Priety, trying to find her everywhere and in every moment results in loosing love once again. I guess I was left with hardly any energy to try to find love again. This time I was promising to never to think of love again.

I was feeling completely void and I just wanted to relax my mind which I couldn't. I was not feeling angry but was feeling something that was neither hurting me nor was it soothing me.

I don't know when I reached Bandra Station, got down from bus and boarded my train. I seemed lost, physically present but lost mentally. The siren was loud and clear and I bid good bye to Pune inside closing my eyes.

"*Excuse me! Is this seat number 32?*"

I was just forced to open my eyes in despair as I looked at the perfect figure standing and inquiring about the seat.

"F-e-a-u-t-i-b-u-l….. I mean beautiful" I said in my mind and kept staring at her.

She gave a strong look through her glasses and again said.

"Excuse me! I guess you are sitting on the wrong seat. This is mine."

Wow! Her voice was as sweet and soothing like Priety's and her glittering eyes through her glasses seemed like Riya's. I was lost again. I apologized and moved on to the next seat.

Wait! wait! Hey guys! I have to be positive and optimistic. Enough of lecture above of not finding love once again. I should try it once again.

"I am sorry, I guess you too are going to Delhi." I asked her starting the conversation.

"Yes I am"

"Hi I am Krishna"

"And I am Shikha"

"Nice to meet you"

"Same here"

:

:

:

:

:

:

"I guess you are Sagittarius or Aquarian........."

Wow! She seemed to be sweet like Priety.

Oh ho! No more past now. Handle the present with love and care. I wish this journey may end up Krishna falling in love once again........